D0962158

ROSE COFFIN

M. P. KOZLOWSKY

SCHOLASTIC PRESS / NEW YORK

Copyright © 2019 by M. P. Kozlowsky

All rights reserved. Published by Scholastic Press, an imprint of Scholastic Inc., *Publishers since 1920.* SCHOLASTIC, SCHOLASTIC PRESS, and associated logos are trademarks and/or registered trademarks of Scholastic Inc.

The publisher does not have any control over and does not assume any responsibility for author or third-party websites or their content.

Library of Congress Cataloging-in-Publication Data available

ISBN 978-1-338-31047-4

10 9 8 7 6 5 4 3 2 1   19 20 21 22 23

Printed in the U.S.A.   23

First edition, October 2019

Book design by Baily Crawford

for Michele
this book, the three before,
and every one after

A GIRL NAMED ROSE

She always knew that one day she would have to conquer the woods or succumb to them. For the first twelve years of her life, Rose Coffin had delayed this moment as best she could. As far back as she remembered, her head had been filled with stories about the strange goings-on in the woods just down the street from her little pink house, across from where she stood every morning waiting for her bus, the bone-chilling noises drifting out like a phantom limb and ensnaring her. The woods were lush and dark and deep, and every inch was covered with dread thick as sap. She had heard tales of human sacrifices taking place within, satanic rituals, murders, disappearances. Late at night there were said to be flashing lights and unusual sounds, exotic smells. Some people were said to lose their minds in there. Some people were said to emerge altered in some way. And some people were said to never have emerged at all.

And now here Rose was, on the precipice of these very woods, about to set foot within. But why?

Because SallyAnn and her friends asked her to. That was why.

SallyAnn had found Rose hidden away in a bathroom stall, quietly singing to herself. She had an oral presentation coming up, and there was nothing Rose dreaded more. She'd rather have her face ripped off by rabid squirrels than speak in front of the class, and the only way to calm herself down was to sing. It was a coping mechanism she had learned when she was little. Her twin brother, Hyacinth, had taught it to her, and for a while, it really worked. But ever since the accident, he wasn't there anymore. And over time, Rose grew quieter and quieter.

"What was going on in there, Rosie?" SallyAnn began. She was taller than all the other girls, her eyes cast down at Rose. "That couldn't have been you singing. I mean, it wasn't half-bad. I'm actually impressed."

Her friends echoed her faint praise.

"So, are you a singer or something?"

Rose's head raised. She was searching SallyAnn's eyes for a motive. A part of her—a very big part—prayed this might be the start of something special. She knew it was dangerous to think like this, but her heart and hopes were pulling the strings now. The words squeezed out of her mouth as if through a pinhole, awkward as ever and directed toward the floor. "Well . . . I . . . Yeah . . . Kind of . . ."

"You know we have a band, right? We're looking for a singer. Care to try out?"

For a year now, Rose had seen flyers for SallyAnn's band all around the school; she had heard the sounds from down the street. It was a beautiful noise. As the question hung in the air, Rose felt faint. If not for the wall, she might have fallen straight back. "M-me?" She knew her face was bright red, and she kept trying to nonchalantly exhale as a way to cool it down.

Rose hated being stared at. Whenever she was stared at, whenever she was embarrassed—which was often and at the slightest bit of attention—her face burned red. It was why she never brought attention to herself, never spoke up for herself, never raised her hand in class—because she would always end up looking like a jar of tomato sauce and someone could always be counted on to point it out, which would make Rose flush even more. She could remember the time way back in third grade when SallyAnn gave her the nickname Rosie because of her fickle pigmentation. It felt like a curse that would never lift. The moment *still* stung, but she always thought that if they ever became friends, the name could be turned around into something endearing.

SallyAnn nodded. "Look, I'm not saying we're going to be besties or anything, but if you can sing the hell out of some songs, you can maybe join our band. It'll be so real." She looked her up and down, her face crumpled as if repulsed. "But if that happens, we'll have to work on your clothes a bit. And that hair. At least run a comb through it."

Rose pulled her unruly hair out of her face. She placed one of her imitation sneakers over the other, as if to hide them, and adjusted her shirt, which was a size too small. These things had caused her tremendous amounts of taunts and ridicule throughout her life—it was as certain as the sun's rise, but with none of the light. But maybe no longer.

"Well?"

"Um, yeah . . . so . . . uh, what kind of music do you play?" she asked, her thoughts running at a wicked pace.

SallyAnn belched laughter. "What, you mean, like, reggae? Jazz? Don't ruin it already, Rosie. Just meet us in the woods after school, okay?"

Hearing this, Rose's stomach flipped. "The woods?"

"Yeah, you know, back where those older boys hang out on their dirt bikes? There. Nobody can know about this, Rosie. You know how jealous some of these girls get. The whole school would be knocking on my door asking for a chance to audition."

But the woods? Rose thought again. *Does it have to be the woods? Does she have any idea what she's saying? Has she ever been in there herself? Has everyone lost their minds?* "Can I . . . I mean . . . Is there anywhere else we can meet?"

"Well, we can all squeeze into that little pink house of yours. Have a look around, see what's in the fridge. How about that?"

She said this with a knowing grin, and Rose went ice-cold. The last thing she wanted was someone like SallyAnn in her house. It would ruin whatever chance they had at being friends. No one ever entered her house, and something told her SallyAnn knew that.

She squeezed the books tight to her chest. "Somewhere else . . . maybe?"

"Be in the woods at four o'clock. Don't make us come knocking." Then, as she and her friends walked out of the bathroom, she said, "And, Rosie, don't be scared. People only die in there at night."

Now, staring into the woods, the previous conversation etched deep into her bones, she understood that her destiny was in her own hands. It was something she could actually control. All she had to do was enter.

Three feet in and she immediately felt cold. It was a warm day in late May, but she swore she could see her breath. Her chest tightened, and her breathing became more and more strained, as if her lungs were encased in ice, as if everything was. Her eyes roamed warily through the woods. All was still and silent. Still and silent and dead.

Don't let the place get inside your head, she told herself. *Just find SallyAnn and everything will be better. For once in your life just have some guts.* Conversation within her head was never a problem. After her brother's accident, the only person she felt comfortable talking with was herself, and she did it often.

Glancing back, she couldn't even see the road anymore. It was like it had been swallowed up. For a moment, it was as if the entire school and all her problems at home were suddenly gone. The woods took her away from it all, and there was a kind of peace in that.

She walked tentatively, her arms wrapped around her gangly body. She had no idea where to go. There were trails, but they veered off in multiple directions. Beneath her chest, her heart was galloping.

Calm down, she told herself. *Calm down or you're going to end up in a ball on the ground. People die like this, Rose.*

People get lost and starve, they fall in a ditch, get eaten by some animal—

"Stop!" she called out. Warily, she glanced around to see if anyone had heard. Then, under her breath, she continued. "Stop it. You're doing the right thing."

After walking awhile down the middle path, she heard a noise, a slow kind of shuffle. "Wh-who's there?" she cried, her voice cracking in a thousand places. Frantically, her eyes tried to locate the source. *SallyAnn? The older kids? That didn't sound like any dirt bike you've ever heard, Rose. Is someone there? Is something following you, Rose? Waiting? Watching? Ready to pounce? You're too young to die!*

If her senses hadn't been numbed with panic, she would have noticed she was whimpering. Her arms were tucked tight against her chest, her hands meeting below her chin, fingers writhing. The sound repeated, and gazing deeper into the woods, she spotted movement. "What is that?" Her head spun at the strange sight, her blood going cold. "S-SallyAnn?" All around her, the trees were moving. Not like if there was a wind—which there wasn't. The branches weren't swaying, the leaves weren't rustling. It was like the trunks had lifted out of the ground and were crawling on their roots toward her, the woods come alive.

It's a mistake, she thought. *An illusion. This is what you always do. Now, stop it. You're not seeing that. You're not!*

Quickly, she hurried down the path, away from the noises and whatever was lurking there.

Eventually, in a small clearing up ahead, she saw splashes of color mixed in with all the green. It was SallyAnn and her friends. They were sitting on fallen trees, laughing and playing around on their phones.

One of the girls spotted her standing there watching them, and nudged SallyAnn.

"Right on time," SallyAnn said, standing up.

Rose was confused. She had been wandering these woods for at least ten minutes. Maybe even fifteen.

"Well, Rosie, don't waste our time. Are you going to sing or not?"

In all the excitement and possibilities of this new life, she had completely forgotten that she had to actually perform. She hadn't sung for anybody in three years. What if her brother had been lying about how good her voice was? What if he had been only looking out for her like he always promised to do? Suddenly, these realizations hit her with the force of a speeding train. "Right. Yeah. Of course." She felt herself wither with insecurity, her voice nothing but weak pops of air.

"Well, let's get on with it."

SallyAnn and the others backed away and Rose shuffled her feet where she stood. Her entire body went numb and her breaths became uncomfortably intense. The heat in her face increased by the millisecond, and her heart provided her with a rapid beat.

She sputtered the first thing that came to her. "'Winter,' by Tori Amos."

SallyAnn and the others looked at one another blankly and shrugged their shoulders, smirking. It was Rose's father's favorite song. She remembered how he used to talk about it, how attentive he was to her, a life long gone now—she sometimes went days without seeing him. Back then, he had Hyacinth learn it on the piano, and when they were alone, Hyacinth taught Rose the vocals. He would play along on the piano, nodding her on with every note—he never smiled so much as when Rose sang. Secretly, in those moments, she always imagined herself as Tori.

Shaking the nerves from her hands, Rose took a deep breath and closed her eyes. She told herself not to open them again until the song was over. *Sing as if Hyacinth's with you. Sing as if he can hear.* For Rose, the song had always been about him anyway.

All at once, her voice broke open, shards of a song cutting a path to the ears around her. *"Snow can wait, I forgot my mittens."*

She heard snickering and her eyes flashed open for a

second. She saw them staring at her, smiles on their faces, their phones out recording everything. With intense fear, she slammed them closed again and continued, her voice still cracking as if it had been encased all this time, but gaining strength with every note, a beautiful ache.

A minute in and the laughter was even louder now. Rose's voice shrank away. She doubted if she'd ever find it again. She opened her eyes to the brutal truth and watched as SallyAnn wiped away tears of laughter, her body hunched over in extreme delight. She pointed at Rose, saying over and over again what a loser she was.

Rose flinched with insult, and her eyes filled with tears and the pain of her life came speeding back. *How could you be so stupid?* she thought. She felt so heavy all of a sudden, lead bones and veins of heavy metals.

"You . . . you never meant it," she said in a slow trickle of a voice. "Not a thing . . ."

SallyAnn straightened up, wiped away one last tear, and stomped her way closer, twisting her left foot into the ground as if putting out a cigarette. "I'm the singer in this band, Rosie. You think we'd ever let you in? We wouldn't even let you carry our guitars. But when we heard you in the bathroom today—oh, man!—had to get that on camera."

Rose was as stiff as the trees around her. SallyAnn circled her like a lumberjack looking for the sweet spot that would bring her down. And what could she do about it? SallyAnn was bigger, tougher, and she had a whole group of friends behind her. Rose had nothing.

The girls kept circling her, zooming in on their phones, cackling and calling her names. For once, Rose was glad her parents couldn't afford to fix her computer or buy her a phone; at least she wouldn't have to read all the comments this time.

SallyAnn folded her arms and cocked her head. "You know why your brother's never gonna wake up, Rosie? The real reason he's in a coma? It's because he doesn't want to see what a loser you are."

Rose felt the tear run down her cheek as if in slow motion and hated with every fiber of her being that SallyAnn saw it.

"Zoom in close!" SallyAnn shouted. "Get those tears in her eyes! Get how red her face is! We're going to plaster this everywhere! What a loser!"

Hollowed, Rose dropped to the ground and curled into a ball as all the girls gathered around. She knew not to get up. She just buried her face and let the tears flow. She felt them kicking dirt on her, putting leaves and debris in her hair. She felt them smearing mud on her jeans as if she had an accident. The jokes and laughter piled up so high she felt crushed.

When they were long gone, fearing the ridicule that would

be awaiting her come the following morning, Rose, crumpled and dirty, turned over to her side and gazed into the woods. As if whispering directly in her ear, the trees emitted a long and strange noise. Whether it was a threat or a lullaby, she didn't know.

Chapter 2
AN ESCAPE INTO
THE WOODS

Inside, the house was so dark and so small and oh so quiet. And so was Rose.

Falling back on her bed, she closed her eyes and thought of the strange feelings that enveloped her in the woods. For a brief moment, it felt like more of an escape than anything SallyAnn could have offered. But even more than that, it felt like some kind of destiny awaiting her.

Stop, she thought. *Get out of your head for once.*

As usual, there was no sign of her father—it was impossible to tell when he would be home anymore. Still, that never stopped her from fingering the necklace he gave her in the hope that might change. Meanwhile, her mother had already come and gone. She was home only long enough to grab something to eat and briefly check in on Rose before heading back out to her evening shift at the hospital, leaving notes around the house for her daughter to find with sayings like "Fight or Succumb." During the day she cleaned houses, but at night she had a custodial job at the same hospital where Rose's brother was staying. Each night, whenever she could, she made sure to move his limbs so that they didn't atrophy; she turned his body on its side so that sores didn't develop. She cut his hair, clipped his nails. She pinched his skin in the hopes he might wake up.

It had been some time since Rose had been to see her brother. The last time she did—the only time—she nearly broke down. She never even made it to Hyacinth's bedside. She had no idea how her mother did it day after day, how she didn't crumble like her husband, and Rose was sorry she couldn't be a better daughter to her. She wished she could be stronger. She wished she could be like her.

＊

Getting up and ready for school was always difficult. The way sleep clung to her eyes, the blankets as heavy as lead, the air snapping at her body and driving her back under covers, if only for an extra minute or two. The irritating shriek of the alarm that dug too deep into her ears, the all-too-slow-to-warm shower, the frustratingly limited choice of breakfast foods. It was all unbearable. And the morning following such a devastating humiliation it was even more so.

Rose tried to lift her backpack, and it felt like an anchor pulling her down. *It wants you to stay*, she thought. *You should listen. The answers are always in the books.*

The air was cool outside, the streets quiet. She headed down her block and to her bus stop opposite the woods, listening to her own footsteps like an ominous metronome. Standing there, she felt as if she had to go to the bathroom. As she rocked back and forth, she knew it was her nerves at play. The bus would be there soon, with SallyAnn on it, and then what? What did that diabolical girl have planned for her today? What was everyone going to say? Did the whole school know what had happened? The more she thought about it, the more she found herself trembling.

The spiking hiss of the bus rounded the corner, puncturing her thoughts. Peering down the block, she saw the bus's nose emerge like a yellow scourge. She imagined SallyAnn sitting in the back, waiting, plotting, her ghouls all around her cackling. Rose picked up her backpack as if it were armor and clutched it to her chest, her heart beating against her books.

As the bus made its sluggish crawl down the long street, Rose stood facing the woods. *But maybe there's something else*, she thought. There was fear in either choice, but she knew she had to act, and if she had done it once, she could do it again. Swinging the backpack over her shoulders, and with the bus bearing down, she raced across the street and darted into the woods.

When she was far enough in, she ducked down and closed her eyes tight, waiting for the bus to pass. Only it never did. At least she didn't hear it. Opening one eye, then the other, she looked out, but she couldn't even see the street anymore. *Weird*, she thought. *These woods must be thicker than they look.* Slowly, she made her way back toward the street, but she never emerged. *Did you get yourself turned around, Rose? Were you not paying attention again?* she wondered. *How far in are you?*

Okay, she thought, trying to remain calm. *There are trails. Trails eventually lead out. Follow the trails, just like yesterday.* Which she did, keeping to the well-worn paths until they eventually didn't lead anywhere. They just stopped. With panic quickly rising up, she backtracked and took an alternate, lesser-traveled route, and nearly a mile later, these did exactly the same.

"Don't get scared. Still better here than in school, right? Right. No SallyAnns here." Using this last sentence as a kind of mantra to keep the fear at bay, she walked for what felt like hours until, finally, she needed a rest. She could feel her body yearning for the magical realm of sleep. Dropping her backpack to the ground, she took a seat on a dry, withered stump, her eyes heavy. No SallyAnns here. Suddenly, she found herself singing "Winter" again, continuing right where she left off. It came easily this time, powerfully. She was louder than she had ever been, her voice crystalizing in the air.

Something dashed past and Rose jumped to her feet, her head caught in a daze. "Who's that?" Nothing moved. There was no sound.

A moment later, something else came dashing by. A deer? Then came another. And another. A dozen of them. They were running so fast, she could barely make them out. But something told her these weren't like any deer she had ever seen. They were . . . different. Bigger. Were their heads red? And the sounds they made . . . no deer cried out like that. But what were they running from?

She turned around, and one of the animals came charging right by her. It flew like a missile and was just as loud, spinning her to the ground. *Did . . . did that one have wings?* She felt the earth rumble beneath her body. Whatever the threat was, it was close. Glancing up, she spotted a huge wall of flames heading her way. Every tree was engulfed, from roots to the highest branches. It stretched as far as she could see, and it moved furiously. Without wasting another second, Rose was off and running with the animals. But as fast as she ran, the fire seemed to be gaining. She felt its heat, the singeing whip of its flames. What if she never found her way out? What if she died in here? *Push, Rose. Move!* Digging deep, she ran harder than she ever had before. Sprinting through the woods, hurtling logs and shrubs, she couldn't believe how fast she was. She was like the deer. *You're going to make it,* she thought. *You're going to survive this thing. You're going to—* And just like that she ran smack into a tree.

Lying on her back, her head felt like it was split open. In fact, she thought she must have knocked herself completely senseless because the tree was moving. It was inching toward her as if on legs, slowly but steadily, until it bent right over her face. "What's happening?" she cried as she tried to scramble away, only to have her escape blocked by yet another moving tree behind her. "What's happening? Somebody help me!" She crawled in a different direction, then another, then another, only to be blocked each time. Her trembling hands dug into the earth and her vision continued to fade in and out as she sobbed, fearing for her life. The world was lit with flames, and the woods had come alive; they were cursed all along, and they had come for her as she always knew they would. The deer continued to stream by as, all around her, more and more trees closed in. And in the middle of them, like a ray of light, was a boy with skin of gold. "This is her," he said. "The one we came for. Take her."

Chapter 3
EPPERSETT

er vision continued to play games. It had to be, because
what she was witnessing couldn't possibly be real.

Apparently she was still too dazed to walk. She thought she
remembered attempting a few steps, but her legs kept buck-
ling beneath her, and now she was being carried. As her
vision returned to her like a slow fade-in, she glanced down at
who was keeping her so high aloft. She seemed to be resting
atop a tree, in a large tangle of branches with odd birds with
purple feathers all around her. But as she peered farther
down, trying to understand how this tree wasn't connected to
the ground, she noticed its trunk was in the shape of a human
body, complete with arms and legs. *That can't be right*, she

thought groggily. *It must have finally happened, Rose. You lost your mind.* Looking ahead, she saw the golden boy leading the way, and the mere sight of him sent a jolt of pain straight through her eyes and into her head as if she had stared at the sun. She quickly realized the only way to safely look at him was out of the corners of her eyes, just like she did with most of the boys at school. He must have been around her age, she figured, and although his skin was gold, he had long dark hair, thick and lustrous, that fell straight down both sides of his face. He walked with great confidence, leading a group of about eight or nine wandering trees through the woods, a sword in a scabbard across his back. He ignored her like every other boy she had ever known, though she clearly never knew one quite like this.

The longer they walked, the more Rose's head cleared; though, like a scar, the confusion and fear remained. Bits and pieces of conversation found her ears, and she nearly screamed when she realized it was the trees talking.

"We found her, that's all that matters!"

"And just in time too! The devastation, I've never seen anything like it! Decades of rebuilding!"

They spoke in loud, gnarled words, the sounds grinding their way deep into her ears.

"Yes, but we'll live!"

"Thanks to her!"

"Thanks to her!" they all echoed.

She had no idea who they were talking about, and she didn't care. Right now she just wanted to get down, and she let them know it. Gripping a branch with both hands, she began to shake it violently, screaming, "Hey! Put me down! Put me down, right now!"

Nobody responded but the birds on the branches, and so she shook the tree some more. "Did you hear me . . . mister?" *"Mister," Rose? Really?* "I want off this thing! I want off this instant!"

Still nothing. Incredulous, she began slamming her foot down on the nearest branch. "Where are you taking me? Help! Somebody, help me! I've been abducted by . . . by an oak! Help me, please!"

She was in such terror, her body overloaded with so much adrenaline, that she snapped the branch clear off the tree. This seemed to get the tree's attention, bringing it to an abrupt halt. In fact, the entire walking forest had gone completely still, as if the crack were a gunshot. Rose, fearing what was to come, began to sink down among the branches. "Umm . . ."

All at once, the limbs around her began to move. Two curled themselves right around her body and lifted her into the air. Soon, she was hovering high off the ground, face-to-face with the tree.

"Why, you could have just asked nicely!" the tree shouted jovially, and he placed her down before him as gently as possible. "I thought you were still passed out!"

Rose had to stretch her neck far to find his face again, he was so tall—his eyes sat nearly eight feet off the ground, but the branches that grew out of his body extended a dozen more feet in all directions. His skin was thick and rough like bark, with the largest branch jutting out of his neck, though there were others coming from his back and stomach, his arms and legs. The strange birdlike creatures that had taken flight at Rose's violence quickly returned to their nests. Although they had red eyes and jagged teeth that hung out of their beaks and wings similar to that of a bat's, they seemed harmless enough. The tree man's beard was moss, his teeth wood. Rose imagined he had been human once and swallowed a seed, the tree taking root within his belly. There were others just like him, though he was the biggest. One of them had a thick branch coming straight out of his mouth, another through an eye, one more through an ear. Some were more like bushes; some were old and withered. It all looked incredibly painful to Rose, enough for her own bones to tighten and ache, but none of them seemed to mind. In fact, the tree wasn't mad; he was downright jolly.

He picked her up in his arms—the humanlike ones, not the branches—hugging her and swinging her from side to side.

"We've been waiting for this day, little girl!" He threw her up, and she nearly pierced herself on one of his branches. She was trembling badly in his arms now, like one of his leaves about to fall. It was one of the only times since her brother's accident that she could remember wishing she were home.

The golden boy hurried forward and demanded Rose be placed back down immediately, while also admonishing the giant tree for his carelessness. "Gentle, Ridge. Where has your head gone? We can't let any harm come to her. She is special. A gift."

For a moment, Rose assumed there must be another girl with them. No one had ever said anything within the same universe of such a compliment to her. Turning to the boy, she couldn't help but beam. Nope. No SallyAnns here. No pink houses. No Coffins. It was like even she had become someone else.

"Of course! Of course!" Ridge shouted, placing her down. "I got ahead of myself! Today is a great day!"

Scrunching her face, Rose wasn't sure he was able to speak quietly. Not that that was her concern right now. Her knees continued to buckle beneath her, she was so nervous, but she had to put that aside. Free from the tree, seeing her chance—perhaps the only one she'd get—she began to run. She made it all of three steps before she collapsed like a house of straw.

The golden boy walked over and helped her to her feet, his hands warm on her arms. "I'm afraid we can't let you go," he said, his tongue as quick as silver. "So you can either walk with me, or go back atop Ridge. The choice is yours."

It was easier to look at him now, as if her eyes only needed time to adjust. He continuously let out deep breaths, this boy, as if his lungs were damaged. There were scars all over his body, she noticed, thick white marks as if the gold were scratched away. He wore heavy brown boots, as well as brown pants and a loose tunic. His eyes were as black as his hair, no iris to be seen. This should have scared her, but she found comfort inside them instead. Looking deep into their centers, she asked, "Where am I?"

With a grin on his face, he walked her a few more steps until they were clear of the woods. The golden boy waved his arm before him and said, "This is Eppersett."

At the end of the woods was a huge cliff, and from there she could see everything.

A great river split the land in two. It was impossibly wide and filled with islands, each one its own city with ships sailing from port to port. Mountains sat in the distance, as far as the eye could see, each one an Everest. They hugged the horizon, extending endlessly in each direction like a natural border. She noticed several castles and forests littered throughout the land, creatures flying through the skies.

There were waterfalls and statues, animals larger than any that had ever walked the earth. And everything was so bright, so colorful, it pained her eyes. Only when she turned her head to gaze behind her did she begin to see something horrific on the horizon. A creeping death. A black wasteland of a sky. *Don't want to be caught in that storm*, she thought, a sinking feeling in her stomach.

"Eppersett," she said to herself, wondering where on earth this place actually was.

The view was so overwhelming, her body could hardly take it. After another few seconds she dropped. Right on her backside. She had to sit down, she had to breathe, to think. Her hands held her head. It was all too much. "I . . . I think there's something wrong. I think I hurt myself really bad." Her hand traced the contours of her skull.

"Don't worry," the golden boy said. "It will all be over soon."

She looked up at him. The words he had used, there was something in the way he said them, something unsettling. Just as she was about to inquire, a hand slapped her back.

"Thanks to you, it will!" Ridge said.

Rose winced at his show of appreciation, but the pain went away quickly as the golden boy placed his hand on her back, a pleasant warmth spreading like blood through veins.

"Don't mind him," he said. "He's quite excitable. All the Willapps are."

"Willapps?"

"These treelike people are called Willapps. There used to be hundreds of thousands of them. But . . . no longer."

"What happened?"

He seemed hesitant and more than a little troubled. His eyes wandered toward the desolation beyond the woods. When they returned, he said, "You don't need to worry about that. You just enjoy these moments."

Rose warmed. It had been so long since she'd had a normal conversation with someone her age. *Well, "normal" being relative,* she thought. In a small voice, she managed to ask his name.

"Coram," he answered. "And I will be at your service these next few days. It is a pleasure to be in your company. Truly." And he smiled at her, a smile that broke her open, her heart bleeding out.

Rose knew she should have been asking him what he meant by "days," what the desolation was—a million important questions—but she suddenly felt light as air, and that included her thoughts too. Maybe it all didn't matter. Maybe Eppersett was where she was meant to be.

Chapter 4
CELEBRATION AT LAMARKA

The group descended down the giant cliff, along an ancient stone staircase built into the rock. As Rose looked down, she was slammed by a wave of vertigo, her head and stomach reeling. Desperately, she grabbed one of the sculptures lining the stairs for balance. There were hundreds of them, each one more confounding than the next. There were scenes and people she could hardly imagine being real, what looked like ogres and sorcerers and dragons. She stumbled down a step or two until she finally sat down and closed her eyes, attempting to settle herself and, more importantly, her stomach. When she felt somewhat calmer, she opened her eyes again and was looking at a statue of what appeared to be a farm girl from decades past. The girl looked valiant and strong, but there was something vulnerable about her too. Almost like she were two people struggling to be one. At the base was inscribed the words: *She who defeated the thousand-headed beast.* Rose meant to reach out and touch it, but for some reason, she found herself touching her own face instead. As she did so, there was a subtle grating sound, and she watched in disbelief as the statue mimicked her pose.

Rose did a double take and stammered, "Wh-what the . . . ?" She looked for Coram to confirm what she just witnessed, but he was already two dozen steps ahead. Stymied, Rose moved again, though this time the statue remained still. *Was it always standing like that?* she wondered.

"Move along now, girly!" Ridge shouted, bumping her forward.

"Did . . . did you see that?" she asked as she was shoved along.

"See what?"

"That statue . . . it moved."

"Naturally!" he said. "Now, come on! Let's keep moving! You act like statues aren't supposed to move or something!"

Begrudgingly, Rose descended the stairs, glaring over her shoulder at the sculpture.

From her high vantage point, she had a good view of much of Eppersett, though very little of it made sense to her. Out in the middle of a large body of water to the west was a series of three towers that, at the top, twisted into one. They were green as if covered in moss and looked to be in ruins. Every now and then, something large, with a very long tail like a crocodile, came shooting out of the water, taking another chunk out of the structures. The towers wobbled, pieces crumbling and splashing into the water. For a second, Rose thought she saw a glowing figure in one of the high windows, and wondered if the monstrous fish was trying to reach it.

Nearly an hour later, the group finally reached the bottom of the cliff. "Not much farther now," Coram said. "Just over that hill." He stopped and looked at Rose, his face contorting. "Do you need a rest? When we arrive, nobody is going to leave you alone. They're all waiting for you as we speak."

To Rose, this sounded like a nightmare, her stomach sinking. "Who is?" she asked.

"Everyone. All of Lamarka."

Rose stopped walking, her legs suddenly dead. Her arms dropped to her sides and she stared ahead, a puzzled look on her face. "What, exactly, is Lamarka?" she asked, her voice very slow, her eyebrows raising higher and higher with each word.

"A city," Coram said. "My home. Come."

Hesitantly, she followed him to the top of the hill, a gentle breeze blowing against her skin, the grass soft, as if each blade were feathers. Pointing ahead, Coram said, "There."

Stretched out before them, hidden in the shadow of the Cliff of Cries, was a small city the likes of which Rose had never seen. Beside the large body of water with the three towers, it sprung from the ground in peculiar shapes, twisting up at unorthodox angles. It wasn't concrete or steel like back home. It was as if the earth itself had manufactured the city. Over what must have been thousands of years, it had grown like a forest, like something living, each and every building unique.

Some were high-rises connected by bridges, and some grew out of the hillside. Some took the shape of massive trees, and some could have been carved out of boulders. Vines and moss ran up the sides and across the roofs of each home and building. The windows and doors were shaped by arched branches. There were animal nests and hanging gardens, stone pathways and balconies. Bright flowers dotted the landscape and miles of ivy slithered like armies of snakes. And above it all, the sky was a magnificent purple, like a beautiful bruise refusing to fade.

Rose gazed out in awe. "It's . . . amazing."

"Funny," Coram said. "They're going to think the same thing about you."

Rose's face grew three shades brighter, and she instantly pulled her body inward as if to hide. She tried not to smile though her lips yearned to, and in a voice that could fit under her nails, she said, "They . . . they don't even know me."

Coram craned his head and found her downcast eyes. "But they know why you're here."

Just as Rose was about to say *she* didn't even know why she was here, a horn blared from within Lamarka, and seconds later, nearly every door and window opened, the population beginning to pour out of their homes, thousands upon thousands of creatures shaking the ground with their eager footsteps.

Just yards from the city's entrance—a huge stone archway carved with the words *Hessop's Gate*—Coram turned to Rose and squeezed her hand. "Are you ready?" he asked.

No. You're not ready. Not at all. "Coram," she asked, "what's this all about?"

"Just . . . just try to enjoy it," he said, only this time it was he who was unable to make eye contact with her.

The moment she entered the city, on a stone path that seemed to grow beneath her feet, Rose began to hear a chant. It started out low, but soon grew to an arena-like pitch, and she realized they were screaming her name. *No . . . way . . .* She wanted to hide. She wanted to dig a hole right then and there, curl into a ball, and disappear. Each chant vibrated through her body, rattling her chest and bones. It shook her weak. Her stomach roiled, edging her closer and closer to sickness. The eyes upon her were like a thousand suns burning her body. She wasn't sure how much more she could take. She wished her brother were beside her.

But Hyacinth wasn't there, and she couldn't hide. She had to face the crowd's attention. And when she did, a very strange thing happened. With every second of boisterous applause that followed, every stamp of their feet and bat of their wings, her little heart began to swell. Even the trees seemed to be crying out for her, the grass, the rocks, the leaves. They loved her. It was genuine. And what began as a nightmare suddenly became a dream, and she couldn't help but radiate like a sun. For these few minutes, she was nothing but pure, positive energy. An unfamiliar smile stretched like a canyon across her face. It was like she was someone else.

Don't get all high on yourself, Rose, she thought, refusing to be lured into another pit of disappointment. *That's exactly what they think—that you're someone else.*

All the strangest creatures she had ever seen cluttered the streets, waving and shouting for her—people floating with wings, people floating without wings; people with two faces, people with animal-like bodies that alternated color with each blink of an eye, people made of glass, people in cloaks. *If they can even be called people*, she thought. There were red creatures and blue creatures, people of copper, people of silver—though none were gold like Coram. They all pushed their way toward her, and the Willapps had to form a barricade, their branches like a fence, keeping Rose safe. All of Lamarka, it seemed, adored her, and for once, Rose didn't want the attention to waver.

Strange music played, something like a natural symphony, as if the earth had taken up its own instruments. Rainbows of flower petals fell from on high, children sat in trees hoping for a better view, and there were even people openly weeping, some whose tears floated upward instead of down.

"I can't believe this," Rose said in a hushed and awed tone, unaware that she was leaning toward Coram, her head practically resting on his shoulder.

"Your kind rarely does."

She looked at him quizzically. "You mean, other humans have been here?"

Coram didn't respond, and at the moment, Rose didn't care; she was so in awe of what she was witnessing. She knew nothing like Lamarka should exist, but she was so overwhelmingly happy it did. If back home were like this, she thought, she would have never wanted to leave.

A group of robed figures stood ominously in a line along a bamboo bridge. Unlike everyone else, not one of them moved or made a sound, and in the darkness of their hoods were the faces of worms, thick brown tubes with black holes in the middle that peered out like periscopes. Coram quickly guided Rose away from them, a shiver down his spine, and toward the center of the city. There, surrounded by flowers taller than she was, loomed a tree so large it shaded nearly every street and alley, and it pulsed with a yellow glow like the city's own star.

Rose was mesmerized by it all, but her gaze was abruptly broken when she was swarmed by the masses. All at once, they came at her. The Willapps were stampeded, most of them pushed back as if by a wave, their branches snapping, except for Ridge, who stood his ground as if taking root. But even he was not enough to keep the crowds at bay. Everyone was reaching for her now. They wanted to touch her hair, her skin. They pulled at her, tugging madly at her arms and clothes.

Ridge tried to keep them all back, but it was no use—the mob began climbing him, weighing him down. He kept yelling, "I don't want to hurt you! Don't make me hurt you!" Coram grabbed Rose in his arms, shielding her with his body. The crowd battered his back and Rose cowered, suddenly quite afraid.

"She's beautiful," someone said, the words squeezing Rose's heart in a pleasurably painful way. "Like I imagined she would be!"

"So unique! One of a kind," someone agreed.

"Our dark days are coming to an end!" another cried.

"You're here! You're finally here! We've waited so long!"

It was strange, the feelings that enveloped her now. There was tremendous fear, for sure, but it was balanced by something she didn't quite expect: exhilaration. "What are they talking about?" she asked Coram through all the madness. "Why are they so happy to see me? I don't understand what's going on! Please, tell me!"

Coram looked at her, slightly confused. "Why, you're going to save their world, of course." Then, with a surprising burst of strength, he plowed through the crowd toward the center of Lamarka. He held Rose by the hand, leading her, but she struggled to keep up. She was still trying to process what he had just told her. It was difficult to even find the words. "I . . . I am?" she said, stammering.

Coram brought her to the city center and pulled her atop a huge platform that extended from the base of the massive tree. From where she was now standing, she could see back in the direction from where they had come, at the darkness she had peered at earlier. Beyond the woods from which they had emerged, the sky was blacker than night and she knew it was the sky of a dying world. It was still very far away, but even so, she could tell there was nothing living beneath it, and that the evil was spreading.

Suddenly, the ramifications of her arrival in Eppersett began to take hold, and a harrowing chill danced across her body. She was no hero. "I . . . I think you have the wrong person, Coram. I can barely take care of myself. How . . . how am I supposed to save anyone else, let alone an entire world?"

"I thought you knew," he said, grabbing hold of her arm, far tighter than he had back near the mob. "Rose Coffin, you're going to save them by sacrificing yourself to the Abomination."

CHAPTER 5
ORDER OF THE SACRIFICE

Whipped up in an ecstatic frenzy, the populace of Lamarka gathered around the platform in the city center, and as they squeezed in by the thousands, the streets rumbled with their presence. Rose felt it in her knees. She could hardly stand, the platform a sea beneath her feet.

"They . . . they want me to . . . die?" The words stumbled out of their own volition. She had little control over anything right now, including the compression of her chest and the weakness in her bones. It seemed she didn't even have control over whether she lived or died.

"No," Coram said, supporting her weight. "They want you to save them."

"By dying!"

Coram looked away, an extra-long breath escaping his lips.

"Why me?" It didn't feel like a sacrifice to her; it felt like an execution. "Why do I have to be the one to . . ." She couldn't even say it. "To . . . to do it?"

Coram answered her simply. "Because it's your turn."

There was a finality to these words that iced Rose's being. She could have been six feet under already. Adamantly, she shook herself free of his arms and glared hard at his dark eyes. "My turn? What's that even mean? I didn't choose this! I didn't even want to come here!"

"Are you sure?"

Rose paused, her head recoiling. *What does he mean by that?* "Well, I'm not doing it. I'm not dying for anyone. Find someone else."

"Only someone from your world can be sacrificed to the Abomination. If there was another way, we would do it. I swear. But only human blood quells the beast. Once the Abomination receives such an offering, it will sleep for a decade, bringing us peace once again."

"But . . . you said it yourself, my death won't even stop the thing. It'll only come back."

"And then we'll do it again. It's the best we can do. It's *all* we can do. The Abomination can't be killed. Not with the magic we have."

Rose shoved him. Her strength surprised her—he went stumbling back several feet, a hand on his chest as if it hurt. For a moment, Coram looked confused, as if he were trying to figure something out. His eyes warily glanced over the crowd, which had collectively gasped, then turned back to Rose.

"Well, I'm not dying," Rose told him. "Not for you, not for them, not for anyone!"

He stepped forward, a little more hesitantly this time. "Don't you want to be a hero, Rose? Look how they adore you."

She didn't even turn her head. She didn't want to think of the eyes on her or how vulnerable she was in this moment. "I don't care."

"That didn't seem to be the case when you first saw them."

A sharp pain ripped through her stomach, like her insides were snared and pulled out, exposing her for what she truly was. "I . . . I . . ." With a rising fury, she forced the feeling aside. "I didn't know they wanted me dead! I thought this place was different. I thought you were different." She exploded into tears.

"Rose . . ." He reached for her hands, but she swatted them away, and Coram flinched as if she wielded a sword.

"I was wrong about you. About it all. Turns out it doesn't matter where I am, people are the same everywhere."

Coram tried to speak, but nothing came out. His eyes

dropped to the floor, his body sagging. It seemed as if he were in great pain.

Oh, don't fall for that, Rose. Not one bit of it. He's as evil as the rest of them. Eyes darting, she searched for a way out of this mess. For a moment, she wasn't sure if she was rotating on the platform or if her world was spinning. Either way, it was clear she was surrounded, the crowd deep and tight on all sides. There was no escaping.

"We need you," Coram said. "Your sacrifice will save millions."

"There . . . there has to be another way." Her voice was distant, feeble, her strength drained.

The deafening chants of the crowd continued to fill her ears. She felt consumed by them, eaten. How quickly it all changed. Her mind was hazy, her body weak. Something wasn't right. Coram moved fast, seizing her by the wrist, his eyes somehow darkening even more. "You will be sacrificed, Rose. You can either accept your destiny like a hero or be dragged to it like a coward."

Horns blasted and through it all Rose's head continued to spin. Drained, she collapsed hard onto the platform. On her hands and knees, attempting to grasp the insanity that had become her life, she followed the sounds and watched as the crowd parted. Something told her there was no way she was getting out of this now. Every passing second was another shovel digging her grave.

Three figures approached the platform, side by side. One looked like a human from the shoulders up, but with an extremely long torso that, a foot above the ground, bent back at almost a ninety-degree angle, with six small legs carrying it forward. It had eight very short arms and a head with drooping red antennae. If she ran, Rose imagined the creature chasing her down, crawling on the ground like a centipede. Beside him—Rose believed it was a him—was a bowling ball of a figure. Nearly completely round, with two large feet and hands protruding and hardly any arms or legs at all, he waddled through the crowd. The smile across his otherwise-featureless face was nearly as wide as he was, with large, perfectly square teeth. Together, he and the centipede fellow were a walking number ten. The third of the group was a female covered in green scales. She had a tail like a dragon, though, similar to the others, her face was human in appearance. She wore a band around her head that was covered in sharp fangs that matched her own.

As they made their way up the platform stairs—the round one bouncing up each step—a hush fell over the crowd. Rose was still on her hands and knees, though now her jaw had joined them on the floor. *Look at them*, she thought. *This is good news. Great news! You're not going to die because this can't possibly be real.*

The dragon woman eyed Rose on the floor before her and, in a reptilian voice, said, "No, sweet sacrifice, we should be bowing to you." And the crowd cheered at this, all of them falling to their knees.

The only way Rose kept from crying more was to laugh. *Ridiculous*, she thought. *This is so ridiculously absurd.*

When the crowd was back on their feet again—Coram helping Rose to rise—the dragon woman continued, addressing everyone. "On behalf of our fearless queen and her long-suffering son—our future king—the great city of Lamarka is proud to have been given the opportunity to offer the sacrifice to the Abomination, bringing us ten years of peace!"

Wild applause. Joyous shouts. Total exuberance. The crowd must have been so desperate for an answer to their troubles for so very long that the cheers lasted nearly ten minutes, until the dragon woman finally raised her hands to silence them.

"The journey to the Abomination is a long and arduous one, with many threats along the way. The sacrifice cannot make it alone. She must be protected, and it is the duty of the citizens of our city to do so. Who of you will risk your lives as the Order of the Sacrifice?"

Immediately, Coram raised his sword into the air, and the dragon woman nodded to him, the crowd applauding with tremendous enthusiasm. "Of course," she said. "Coram Sepsix, our bravest warrior. I never suspected any less." Gazing out to the crowd, she asked, "Who will join him on this quest?"

"Where the boy goes, I go!"

Rose followed the familiar voice and spotted Ridge making his way through the crowd, many of his branches broken or snapped off, some still dangling, the birds clearly irritated. Still, he was beaming his usual smile as if this was all a game. He joined them on the platform, slapping Coram hard on the back. Leaning into Rose, he said, "I'll make sure the Abomination gets you alive, dear girl! Don't you worry about that! You'll be breathing full and wide awake when it puts you in its giant maw!" Rose shot him a look of utter disbelief and contempt, and the big tree guffawed. "I will! I promise!"

Clearly pleased, the dragon woman folded her hands. "Any others?" she asked. "There must be more brave souls out there."

The crowd looked nervous, as if they might be called on for such a mission. As much as they yearned for peace, none of them wanted to risk their lives to achieve it. There was a long and deep silence before a sharp howl cut through the air. Nightmarish and cold, the sound chilled Rose to the bone. She imagined it could only be a product of something incredibly evil, and she had no desire to find out what it was. Yet, to her surprise, what she saw coming through the crowd was hardly menacing at all. It was a large doglike creature with short brown-and-black fur and clear and playful eyes. The animal with the sweet face shambled forward, standing a good four feet tall—if it stood on its hind legs it would be taller than most humans—and while its tail was slightly longer than a dog's and its teeth slightly sharper, its nose was massive, sitting on the end of a long snout like a beehive on a branch.

There was something in the animal's mouth too—a rope or leash—and Rose quickly realized that this creature wasn't the one that howled. It was pulling forth another of its kind. As she heard a second howl, Rose braced herself, her body heavy with dread. The second beast was nearly twice the size of the first. It strode through the crowd like a king, its head held high, lips caught in a snarl. It was mostly white, the fur all ragged with many scars. There was a slight limp, and an ear was missing, but there was no mistaking the beast's majesty. It was very old and, staring at its white eyes, Rose realized it was also very blind. The first animal led the other to the stairs and, together, they made their way onto the platform, each as different as night and day.

When they reached the dragon woman, the blind one spoke in a terrible and cold voice. "I will ensure this mission's success. You have my word, Bethesda."

The dragon woman nodded. "The great warrior Deedubs, we cannot thank you enough. You and your son."

"Eo is just a guide," Deedubs sneered. "Good for nothing more."

Rose watched as the lead animal's eyes dropped, his head sinking. She also caught Ridge shifting away from the feared beast as it approached.

Another minute passed and no one else was stepping forward. Glancing to her left, Rose didn't think it was much of a group—maybe she could even find a way to escape them at some point. They had to sleep, didn't they?

"Is that all?" Bethesda, the dragon woman, asked the crowd. "Is there no one else?"

"I will join them!"

Everyone turned their heads in the direction of the voice, including Rose. She could tell someone was trying to elbow their way through the masses, but the people refused to budge. Whoever it was, they didn't garner the same respect Deedubs did. Not even close. They didn't want this person anywhere near the platform.

Finally, however, the figure managed to push through. It was a short and stocky young girl with a mess of purple hair— Rose wondered if it was always like that or if the crowd had gotten to it. The girl strode forward with force, her shoulders barreling forth, her hands in tight fists. As the people called her a traitor or a disgrace or a joke—there was also a lot worse—she just pushed on, a scowl on her face, her boots stomping the ground. Rose noticed that she had wings on her back, but they were cut almost to the stumps. If she had once been able to fly, she never would again.

The girl reached the platform and, forgoing the stairs, jumped to the surface, a height of nearly eight feet.

"I will see that peace befalls us once again!" she shouted, and everyone howled with laughter. The crowd started up in their mockery again, objects were thrown, but Bethesda calmed them with a simple wave of her hand.

"This will not buy you redemption, Meadowrue," she said, speaking, it seemed, for everyone. "Your sins can never be forgiven."

Meadowrue stared her down. "I'm not seeking redemption or forgiveness. And I don't want praise either. I don't want anything. I have skills to offer, and that's what I'm doing. You have a problem with that?"

Bethesda stared at her, and Rose wasn't sure if she was angry or startled or both. Finally, she said, "Very well."

Meadowrue stepped over toward Rose and gazed at her. Gazing back, Rose thought she saw something in her that might connect them. A common ground, a shared history of pain and isolation. *Finally*, she thought, *someone who will get you.* She offered a slight smile, and in response, Meadowrue said, "If you don't cooperate, I'll eat you myself."

Rose swallowed hard and turned away. *Then again, maybe not.*

Bethesda waved her hand at the group and said, "Then we have our Order. There is no time to waste—you must depart at first light. As you know, the Abomination destroys at an unfathomable pace. Good luck." She approached Rose and placed her hands on her shoulders. "And you, Rose Coffin, will not be forgotten. Thank you for your sacrifice."

"But . . . but . . ."

The dragon woman abruptly turned around. As she rejoined the two she arrived with and walked across the platform and down the steps, the round one, in a balloon of a voice, added, "I wonder how she tastes."

Chapter 6
A LONG NIGHT
IN LAMARKA

Because she had refused to budge from the platform, Rose was stuck atop Ridge once more, his branches the bars of her cage, the birds her wardens. *Apparently,* she thought, *you're going to exit this world the same way you came into it.*

Night was coming on quick—far quicker than it had any right to, as if it just fell atop them—and she was carried through Lamarka toward an isolated place in the Craven Hills section of the city, which had been set aside for her to sleep. According to Coram, it was an area full of history with many sacred areas and landmarks. He went on about devils without tails, the Alder Church and ghost priests, but Rose was having none of it. Sitting atop Ridge, she was like a

48

trapped animal scurrying to break free of her cage. Her chest was thumping, her face panic-stricken, as she kept trying to climb down from the tree at every chance, cutting her hands and legs along the sharp, writhing branches only to be ensnared again and again. At one point, she even attempted to jump, but the branches, like tentacles, snatched her out of midair and pulled her back in, setting her high in the tree.

"I don't want to tie you down!" Ridge shouted up to her as the rest of the group laughed at her feeble escape attempts. "Those branches wrap tight! Don't fight it! Be like a rose and stay in one place, why don't you!"

"Like a tree?" she snapped, which elicited even more laughter from the group.

Rose, however, heard none of it. With her back against the branches, hands grasping two thick boughs, she trembled with a mix of rage and terror. The beauty of the land was gone. Nothing shimmered, nothing shined. At night, it seemed, the demons came out in full. The shadows danced, twisted images and withered figures making all kinds of sounds, snorts and squeals, gasps and croaks. From her high vantage point, she spotted the robed worms slowly trailing the group in a single file, arms folded before them, hands hidden in their billowing sleeves, their heads bowed. If she knew what the Balbot Sect actually wanted of her, she might have preferred being captive in Ridge's branches. Luckily, Coram and

Meadowrue spotted them as well and, after a long conversation with the sect, of which they minimally informed Rose, managed to drive them off.

After many meandering paths through the narrow Lamarkan streets, the group entered a field of rolling hills, eventually stopping at a small wooden door carved in the side of a steep slope. As the Order was arguing about who was going to sleep in beds that night and who was going to keep watch outside the room, Ridge reached up and placed Rose down. "Go get yourself some rest!" he said. "It's been a long day!" But as he opened the door for her to enter her new quarters, guiding her inside with a gentlemanly bow and wave of his hand, Rose had already taken off.

She knew that once Ridge got the others to stop arguing long enough for him to alert them of her escape, they would gain fast, particularly the doglike creatures. There was no way she would outrun them. Instead, she was going to have to find a place to hide. But glancing around, she saw there was nothing but hills.

At the top of the highest hill, she noticed a few small streets in the distance below. With no other options, she decided she'd head there. Racing down the hills, nearly tumbling head over heels, she soon reached the quiet neighborhood. Glancing back, she could see her pursuers at the peak. She'd have to hurry, though it turned out the streets were cobblestone, forcing her to be more sure-footed and slower than she preferred—once or twice she felt her ankle twist and her knees buckle. Still, it felt like she was flying, her strides long and powerful. She wasn't sure if it was the product of fear and adrenaline, and she didn't care. She was just happy to see no movement behind her, nor hear any sounds of people giving chase. She smiled, rounded a corner, and ran straight into the Balbot Sect. She crashed into them as if they were a concrete wall and fell backward, her head smashing against the cobblestone. There were seven of the hooded worms standing over her, motionless and silent. Rose backed away, and two of them lit up, bright red. Beams shot out of their hoods and sleeves, a strange vibration coming from them, a deafening hum, and Rose leapt to her feet and took off in the opposite direction, her scream stuck in her throat like a spike.

Racing down the street, she tried opening every door she passed, but they were all locked. She pounded on some, kicked others, but kept running, never looking back. Finally, just as she was about to give up hope, she threw herself against a door and it flung open.

She couldn't believe it was unlocked. But then she saw the lock was broken, as if someone had ripped it off. She leaned against the door, her body slumping down, putting all her weight against it. The room was dark and quiet. Small. Only enough space for a tiny kitchen and a bed. A square table and two chairs. There was a smell that turned her stomach. In the far corner where the bed was, she heard someone breathing. But it wasn't normal breathing. It was strained, troubled breaths. *Don't wake up, don't wake up.* Slowly, she rose, inched over to the window, and peered out to see if the Sect or Order had passed.

Everything seemed quiet until . . .

"Heeelllppp meee."

Nose against the windowpane, Rose went ice-cold. The voice was fractured, shards of syllables stretched out into a kind of monstrous song. She couldn't move, not an inch.

Behind her, the bed creaked and she heard it again. "Help meeeeeee." Slowly, Rose turned from the window. By the faint light of the moon, she saw a ghostly figure approaching. He was deathly pale. Like his body was dipped in white paint. He kept making his way toward Rose, feet dragging across the floor, one larger than the other.

Rose backed away toward the door, her fingers grasping the handle. She turned it but heard a commotion out in the street. *Shoot!* Rose thought her body was going to crumble. It felt so loose, so wobbly. The pale man kept coming toward her.

"It got me," he groaned, his voice wrapped in a deathly rasp. "I'm sick. Help me."

"Wh-what got you?"

The pale man's hands grabbed her shoulders and squeezed. He looked her up and down, scrutinizing every inch. "What are you?"

Rose's eyes narrowed, and she shoved him away.

"You're not one of us," he said, staggering. "You're not from here. Are you . . . are you her? The sacrifice?"

"No," Rose said. "No. I'm just trying to find my way home."

"Help us!" he moaned. "Pleeaassee!" And he lunged for her.

Rose leapt out of the way, falling to the floor and rolling toward the window. The pale man turned for her, stumbling in her direction.

Just then the door was kicked open and Coram hurried in. He scanned the room and grabbed hold of the man, forcing him back to the bed. "You slipped your cuffs," he said to him in a voice far calmer than Rose expected. He almost sounded like a parent caring for a child. "The illness is eating away at you, Grenenbare." Releasing a deep breath, he eased the man onto the bed and gently placed his hands through the cuffs, tightening them. "It's for your own good. We're going to fix this, I promise. I'm going to see it through. Now just rest." He placed the blanket over him, tucking it in just beneath his chin.

Rose was crumbled on the floor, vibrating with fear and shock and confusion. Coram approached her, his hands up in peace. Crouching beside her, he gently helped her to her feet, though Rose immediately shook him off.

"What was that?" she cried when they were back on the street.

"A good Lamarkan suffering a horrible fate."

"Good? None of you are good!"

Coram exhaled. "It's the Abomination, Rose. It infected him and thousands of others far south from here. He lost everything. It's a miracle he even made it back to us. But the disease is killing him now. Like it's doing to all of Eppersett. The land and the people alike."

"Maybe you deserve it," Rose snipped.

"You don't know what you're saying. You know nothing of suffering."

Rose, surprising herself, slapped him across the face. She was trembling, but she wouldn't look away. "You don't know me," she said through a stiff jaw. "You have no idea what I've lost."

Coram glared back at her—it was clear he had never been treated in such a way. Finally, he said, "Let's get you back to your bed. You're far too important to be wandering around at night."

He and the group brought her back safely to the door in the hill. It was agreed they would take turns sitting outside the door. But the shifts weren't easy for any of them. Throughout the night, they heard nothing but the sound of Rose's tears.

CHAPTER 7
FIELD OF STYLITES

The following morning, the Order of the Sacrifice had been followed out of Lamarka by a wave of raucous applause. There were plenty of well-wishers trailing the group along the wide stone path and out through Hessop's Gate, though Rose supposed in her regard they were more like death-wishers. Spirits were high, save for hers, of course. Escape seemed impossible. Even if she did manage to get away, they would most likely track her down before she found a way back home. She had to face it: She would never see her family again. And what would that do to her mother? Her father? What would that do to Hyacinth?

You've already let him down, she thought. *You can't bear to even be in the same room with him. Because you're scared. Well, how do you think he feels?* It was hard to think of Hyacinth being afraid. He never was. He was always so strong, whether he was defending her from bullies or taking the blame when they broke their father's bowling trophy or just making sure she was never alone. But the more Rose thought about this, the more she wondered if he really was strong. Maybe he was just strong for her. Maybe she still needed him to be. *If he were here, Rose, he'd help you get home.*

The moment the crowds were gone, the arguments among the Order, initiated the night before, began in earnest. To Rose, it seemed like some things were quite common in both worlds.

"I'm leading this group," Deedubs said, shaking his leash so that Eo would guide him to the front, briskly passing Coram and Ridge, who were busy discussing the best route to take.

"Look at you," Meadowrue said. "You can't even lead your-self." She showed no fear, not even when Deedubs bared his teeth and growled in her direction—it wasn't even meant for Rose, but every hair on her body stood on end.

"You think it should be you, do you?" he asked. "The girl who has been cast out of every town she's lived in? The girl whose entire life has been one bad decision? No one would follow you anywhere, Meadowrue. You shouldn't even be here with us. You are a risk, a plague."

Meadowrue's face remained impressively stoic. Not even her body language changed. Rose imagined this was a girl who had heard such comments and faced such threats often, and then some. It must have been so constant that it all rolled off her now. But was that even possible? Every name Rose had ever been called echoed in her still. Every poor decision she made, every moment of being bullied, was still ringing in her ears like a siren. It wasn't easy to shake these things off; in fact, she was still stinging from what Coram had said to her the night before. How did this girl do it? *And she's so young too*, she thought. *She can't be much older than you. How did she get so strong?*

"Tell me," Deedubs went on, his voice like gravel, "in Stammandy, how many innocents died because of you, how many families, how many children?" He dug into the questions, scooping each word up onto his long, rough tongue and letting them rumble out his mouth.

There was the tiniest of flinches, and it was all in Meadowrue's eyes. But something told Rose the interrogation had struck her painfully hard. And whatever burdens Rose had felt all her life suddenly seemed so light.

With her hands gripping her two short blades, Meadowrue took a powerful stride toward Deedubs and, as if he could see her coming, the blind beast lowered his front legs, ready to pounce.

Rose almost wished for a fight, thinking it might provide enough of a distraction for her to escape. Instead, for the first time, Eo spoke up, and Rose suspected it wasn't to protect his father or Meadowrue, but to save the mission. His voice was almost exactly how Rose figured it would be: deep and soft like a pillow, with a strange and hesitant locution, nothing like his father's. "Um, maybe, Pa, I dunno, we don't need a leader, and stuft. Maybe we can all just work together. Maybe. And stuft. You know?"

Turning his head, his father followed his nose and found his son close by. "You're no warrior!" he barked directly into Eo's ear. "You have no say!"

Whimpering, Eo cast his eyes downward. "No, you're right, Pa. You're right. Um, I forgot and stuft. Sorry."

"No, he's not right," Coram said.

Deedubs's ears perked and his head snapped toward the new target of his ire. "What did you say, boy?" Rose had no doubt the beast would take them all on at once if he had to.

Though Deedubs couldn't see him, Coram stood tall, chest out, chin high. For the moment, his deep exhalations ceased.

"I said you're not right. We're all risking our lives on this journey and that means we all have a say. I second Eo."

"Third!" Ridge shouted.

The fur on Deedubs's neck was spiking. "Have you no respect? No sense of living history? I have fought to keep this land safe for nearly two centuries now. It was I who brought down the Stone King. It was I who led the Thin Man's army in the Battle of the Fallen Comet. From the day I was born, I have witnessed things that would strike you blind well before you ever reached my age, boy. This world has been in constant peril, and I have consistently kept that danger at bay. You are nothing but a pup, Coram. Like my pathetic boy. I know what we are facing. I know what we need. And none of you have it."

Silence gripped the group, the tension palpable. They were not even a mile from Lamarka, and already the loose thread had been pulled taut.

"What does the sacrifice think?" Ridge asked in his bellowing voice, shattering the silence like it was glass. His eyes drifted up toward her. "Hello, up there! What say you?"

Rose looked down, incredulous. "What say me? I mean I? What say I?" She closed her eyes and shook her head in frustration. "I say you take me home this second. That's what I say."

"Speak up, girl!" Ridge said. "Why do you always speak so low?"

"I said, take me home!"

"Your home is in the belly of the beast," Deedubs said in snarling dismissal.

"Well, you certainly don't get my vote," Rose mumbled in return.

Eo laughed at this and, a second after he did, he must have realized what he had done. His expressive brown eyes grew wide, his long, floppy ears pulled back, and it was as if he wanted to shove the laughter back down his throat. He couldn't even turn toward his father, who was growling something fierce.

"Careful, little sacrifice," Deedubs said to Rose. "I don't share the awe for you that everyone else does. To me you are meat and nothing more."

Rose was sharply aware of the dangerous ground—*or branch*—she was currently on, but she didn't care. Somehow, even held captive as a sacrifice, she felt stronger than she had ever been. Perhaps it was this place or, more likely, it was the cold force of facing certain death, but whatever it was, she found a source of courage that had never before existed within her. "I think you're losing your mind in your old age, Dubsy."

All Deedubs's teeth were showing now. "Watch yourself, girl."

Rose stood taller than she ever had. "Something tells me you're not what you used to be."

Then it all happened so fast, though Rose saw it before anyone else did. Deedubs's head reared far back, and a deep howl escaped from his bowels. In an incredible flash of movement, he leapt toward Ridge—thirty feet through the air—landing high in his branches. The birds scattered as he snarled and snapped his teeth at Rose like a rabid beast.

Everyone was shouting, but all Rose felt was panic. Whatever bravery she previously had was now gone. Suddenly, she felt weak and helpless and frightened, like the little girl she had always been. All that surprised her now was how she was able to climb so high in the branches so fast. Growing up, she had always seen kids climbing trees, and yet whenever she'd tried, she never once made it past the first branch. Now here she was scaling branches like a squirrel.

Deedubs scrambled for a foothold, his legs kicking out, breaking branches, while, beneath him, Ridge staggered to and fro for balance. "Whoa! Whoa!"

Rose, pale with terror and with nowhere else to go, gazed down at the crazed animal, his nose pulsing as he searched for her scent. His jaws opened unbelievably wide. *He can swallow you whole, Rose. What were you thinking?* The branch she stood on was thin and bending, her feet just inches from Deedubs. She hoped it would hold.

On the ground, Coram ran toward the leash that had been ripped from Eo's mouth. He wrapped it around his hands several times; then, with a tight grip, he yanked hard, and Rose watched as the rope constricted around Deedubs's neck. A second later, he went crashing down through the branches and onto the hard ground.

"Enough!" Coram yelled, his sword drawn, the tip digging into Deedubs's neck. The animal was on his back, paws in the air, frozen. "Another move in her direction and my blade plunges deep. You understand me?"

Deedubs's long tongue lashed out. "She is vaunted as the sacrifice, and yet she knows nothing of surrendering herself for the betterment of others. I've sacrificed all my life—I've sacrificed my own eyes—and what has it gotten me? This? Disrespect? A sword at my throat?"

"Are you going to risk everything over your ego, Deedubs? We need her alive. You know this."

Growling, Deedubs nodded. Coram sheathed his sword, and the beast flipped over and stepped back. "I wouldn't have killed her," he said. "Just taken a leg or two, like meat on a bone."

"We need her whole," Coram said.

"Maybe so," Deedubs answered. "But we don't need you to be. You pull your sword on me again and I will tear you to pieces."

"My people have killed many Cobberjacks in our day, Deedubs. I am late getting started. You can always be my first." Before the Cobberjack could respond, Coram addressed the rest of the group. "As for a leader, we lead with the best idea. Whoever has it, in that moment they're in charge. Every second we waste arguing is another second in which someone dies. The Abomination is southeast from here. That gives us two paths to take. One, across the Sunken Plains, and two, through the Field of Stylites. Any suggestions?" He looked around, waiting for a response, but his eyes drifted up toward Rose. He nodded at her as if to ask if she were okay.

With her legs finally sturdy enough, Rose climbed lower in Ridge's branches, nodding softly in return, eyes quickly darting away. *Don't go all "my hero" on me, Rose*, she immediately thought. *Don't think for a second he cares if you're okay. He's just hoping you still look appetizing enough to serve.*

Meadowrue spoke up, her eyes on the horizon. "The Sunken Plains are treacherous. How many have been lost to the Underdwellers there? Their traps litter the landscape, and the screams of the captured ring out still. We should go through the Field of Stylites instead. It's faster and safer and, with their knowledge, they may have an exact location of the Abomination."

As Deedubs sniffed in contempt at the suggestion, Coram

smiled. "Good thinking, Rue." He waved an arm before him. "Lead the way."

Meadowrue stepped forward, a look of hesitation on her face that said she was surprised that she would be leading anyone.

But lead she did, with Rose above her still shaking like a leaf on Ridge's branches.

✳

The Field of Stylites was more east than south and, according to Coram, even after a seven-mile hike across some lasting hills outside Lamarka, still a long distance away. Plenty of time for Rose to consider her impending fate. With the swaying of the branches gently rocking her like a child in a cradle, the birds' song in her ears, she recalled the old nursery rhyme. It always sounded like a dark and cryptic little lullaby to be singing to babies, but it suddenly felt very appropriate to her. She imagined the bough breaking beneath her and herself falling right into the open maw of the Abomination. Such a chilling vision had her bolting upright, heart pounding. She gripped the branches tight, checking their durability, a cold sweat breaking out on her forehead.

Over the hills and across the valleys, Coram made sure to keep close to Ridge, his eyes continually drifting up toward Rose. He seemed agitated, as if struggling with something.

At one point, after making eye contact with him, Rose, fed up with the wild speculation in her head, asked, "What, exactly, is the Abomination?"

"You really want to know?" Coram asked.

She wasn't sure she did, but she nodded anyway.

"It's a monstrous thing," he said, shaking his head as if in disbelief. "All black, like it's covered in sludge. Dripping, oozing. Eight skittering legs. Massive too. So I've been told, anyway—not too many people have witnessed it and lived to tell. It has a long snout that it plunges deep into the ground. And when it does this, the surrounding land is destroyed. Somehow the Abomination dries it right up, dead, like it's sucking Eppersett's lifeblood or something. And every time it does this, it grows even larger. I imagine it's hundreds of feet tall by now and who knows how long? And the bigger it gets, the stronger it gets, the more death and destruction it spreads. It brings storms with it, and every few days it grows monsters out of its back."

Rose's eyes were wide, and she once again felt sick to her stomach.

"You see why we're so desperate," Coram said. "If you hadn't come along, the Abomination would devour this entire land in only a matter of time."

"So glad I can be of help."

Coram, shoulders slumping in shame, glanced at Meadowrue as if for assistance. She was far ahead of the group, walking very cautiously, her swords drawn. Rose noticed she was always on her toes, ready for battle, and with little time for idle chatter. Deedubs and Eo, meanwhile, were not far behind her. After assessing his group's status, Coram said in a weak voice, "Rose, I know you must be scared." He glanced sideways at Ridge, aware that his old friend was the only one who could hear the compassion he currently let slip.

"Who, me?" Rose answered. "No. This is how I always dreamed of going out. Real martyr-like."

"I wish there was another way. Truly. When the time comes, I promise you I will not be celebrating like the others."

"That warms my heart," she said. "Truly."

Lowering his head, Coram kicked at the ground. "I wish you could see it my way. One life will save millions."

"Then how about we trade places? How's that sound?"

Coram looked wounded, and Rose straightened along the branch. She had never spoken like that to anyone, never really stood up for herself, and it felt really good. A small victory.

After composing himself, Coram said, "If I could switch with you, I would. In a second."

"Oh, I'm so sure."

"Aye, he would," Ridge said. "I never met a soul with more honor than Coram Sepsix!"

"Yeah, well, the honorable thing would be to not sacrifice anyone. To find another way."

Coram looked as if he were struck. He stumbled a bit, his hand leaning against Ridge's trunk of a body. When he regained his composure, he slowed his pace until he was walking alone, head down, his hair hiding his face in shame.

"Sensitive lad," Ridge said to Rose. "But when the time comes, he always does the right thing! I remember the day the great warlock Weskind went mad, by a spell of his very own no less, and he began setting ablaze just about everything in sight, and Coram—"

"Ridge . . ."

"Yes?"

"Shut up."

The Order traveled along many hills, several of them rising and falling as if they were alive—Ridge said this was only somewhat true—while a little later on, a dust storm appeared out of nowhere. Not a thing could be seen through it, but objects kept slamming into Rose, nearly knocking her out of the tree. She heard them hitting every branch around her. And when the storm passed, Eo and Deedubs had furry, spindly-legged creatures in their mouths and two were sliding down Meadowrue's swords. They were called dust flies, and this was what the group ate—all except for Rose, who was starving but convinced herself she still had her dignity.

Eventually, the land flattened out for good, sand over-taking everything, and Rose could see hundreds of pillars in the shimmering distance. There appeared to be figures atop many of them, though not one was moving. In the blazing heat, they sat as still and silent as can be.

"Who are they?" Rose asked as the Order neared.

"Those are the Stylites," Ridge said. "Seers of our land!"

"They never come down from the pillars," Coram said. "Their entire lives are spent up there. Morning, noon, and night. Day after day. Year after year."

"What for?" Rose asked, bewildered as to why anyone would ever do such a thing.

"They seek the answers we all yearn for. Life's mysteries are clear to them. They are wise beyond belief and at peace with the world. Not even death can faze them."

Rose gazed ahead at the Stylites, wondering what kind of dedication this took. The figures were all incredibly thin, their skin a sickly yellow. They sat on stone pillars of varying height, none smaller than eight feet, some of them intricately carved with strange symbols and mysterious images. There were baskets tied to ropes beside them, but how often did people come along bearing gifts of bread and water to fill them with? Rose looked around as if she might find an answer, but they were in the middle of nowhere, not another soul in sight.

The Stylites all had red sheets over their faces, hanging down just past their chins. She saw the fabric clinging to their mouths and noses, revealing a skeletal silhouette beneath. The sun beat down on their backs—no place to hide. Was peace only found through suffering? If that were the case, would she ever find it herself?

The group walked through the field, and not one of the Stylites peered out from beneath their sheets. Not one stirred or coughed or asked who was there. It was an eerie feeling, like being among the dead. Rose, sitting high up in Ridge's branches, her eyes nearly level with the Stylites, glanced into the sky. There were large birds circling overhead. Though, if she were being honest with herself, they looked more like dragons.

"Keep moving," Deedubs said. "The Stylites have nothing to offer us. They've been sitting up there all my life and for generations before that. They never contributed anything to this world. Wastes of life, all of them."

"Pa, everyone has something to offer and stuft, right?"

"Of course they do. Plenty offer an abundance of aggravation and disappointment. A burden I am quite aware of."

Eo shook his ears as if he didn't want the words lingering in them. Then, dropping the rope from his mouth and looking up at the top of one of the pillars, in utter defiance of his father, he said, "Um, excuse me? Um, can we ask you a question and stuft?"

The head of the nearest Stylite slowly turned in Eo's direction. After a hauntingly silent moment, it let out a strange high-pitched moan that froze Rose's blood. Very quietly, she shifted down a few branches while Eo whimpered and stepped a foot back, his ears and head low to the ground. The others encouraged him on, but his tail was now well between his legs. It was clear his father smelled his fear, and Rose felt pity for the peaceful animal.

Coram stepped forward instead, his neck straining to see the top of the pillar. "We . . . we seek the Abomination," he said, and Rose was surprised to hear fear in his voice, not that she blamed him.

A long arm came up very slowly. A crooked finger extended, the nail long and sharp.

"That way?" Coram asked. "To the south? Through the Mid-Lands? How far has it reached?"

That awful sound again. Rose feared she would never be able to get it out of her head.

"That's . . . that's horrible," Coram said. "But we come bearing the sacrifice."

Even with the sheet over the Stylite's head, it was able to find Rose. It seemed to stare at her from beneath, its breathing increasing until it appeared to be convulsing.

When it finally settled down, with a voice like a storm of knives, it said, "She is not who you think. She is the Unwonted."

Excuse me? What now? To Rose it sounded like "unwanted."

Coram's eyes darted from the Stylite to Ridge to Rose and back. He looked confused, shocked, and doubtful all at once.

"I told you," Deedubs said. "They are worthless. Driven mad by sun and starvation and questions that will never be answered."

As if seeking payment, the Stylite lowered his basket, the chain rattling against the stone of the pillar.

Deedubs's ears perked up at the sound. "For what?" he said, aghast. "Coram, don't you dare give it a thing."

But Coram reached into his bag regardless and placed several items into the basket, including chunks of the leftover dust flies. The Stylite lifted it back up, searched its contents, then said, "Something has come for you."

"What do you mean?" Coram asked.

"The Abomination knows of your arrival. It has sent satellites, and they are near. They wish to kill all of you."

Chapter 8
A CONJURING

Coram immediately unsheathed his sword, and Meadowrue her two. Beside them, Eo unleashed Deedubs, and Ridge smacked his fists together, a grin still on his face. Rose, meanwhile, quaked.

"What's he mean?" she asked, her voice as twisted as Ridge's branches. "Who wants to kill us?"

"The creatures I told you about," Coram answered as he rotated in a tight circle, waiting for any sign of them. "The ones that grow on the Abomination's back. Somehow they've found us."

"We've been tracked," Deedubs said. "Hunted. I can smell them. There're at least a dozen."

"They never travel in groups that big," Meadowrue said.

"Aye," Ridge answered. "It's as if something led them to us!"

Glancing around, even Rose knew the Field of Stylites was no place to fight—they were closed in with little room to maneuver and poor visuals, the pillars cutting off all sight lines. But they were in far too deep to run out for open space now. They'd never make it.

From her high vantage point, Rose thought she spotted something leering out at them from behind a pillar about forty yards out. Whatever it was standing there, it was pure white. Like a blank space upon which the world hadn't been filled in yet. In fact, she couldn't even be sure there was anything there at all. A glare of the sun, perhaps? With her heart beginning to beat faster, she leaned forward, her eyes narrowing for a better look. "What the—?" Her throat closed up at the sight, and her body went cold. A gaping black hole appeared in the middle of the white, and with a tumble of dread in her stomach, Rose realized it was the creature's mouth. It had opened and inside was black—she could see the white teeth contrasted against the midnight pitch. Soon, the creature's eyes became noticeable too, a white iris in a pool of darkness. There were black slits for its nose, little dark spirals for its ears. *It's all black on the inside*, she thought. *Dead.*

"Coram?" she said through a choke. "Coram?"

But he didn't answer. Sweat had broken out across his golden brow, and his eyes were darting nervously back and forth, his breathing rapid. Everyone was crouched, ready to fight, while, above them, the Stylites sat motionless, and above *them*, the dragons, which were clearly scavengers, flew in faster and faster circles, anticipating the upcoming battle and its many casualties.

Something ran past—a streak of light—moving from pillar to pillar. Rose could hear the patter against the sand. Whatever it was, it moved fast.

"Stay close," Coram told the group. "Don't let them pull us apart. We split up among these pillars and we're all dead. Everyone stay—"

Meadowrue was slammed face-first to the ground, a screen of dust billowing up all around her. Even with a busted nose, she held on to her swords, but her eyes were panic-stricken as they gazed out helplessly upon the group. Through the mist of sand and with a terrible shriek, something had grabbed hold of her legs and dragged her off into the field. It all happened so fast and so violently, Rose could only clutch her heart in horror and scream as she watched Meadowrue disappear.

"Rue!" Coram called. "Rue!"

"We have to go after her!" Ridge cried.

"Stay where you are. The girl's already dead," Deedubs said. "And if you go, you will be too. Along with the sacrifice."

Nobody spoke, their eyes searching one another's for an answer, though none came. Rose kept expecting to hear Meadowrue cry out, but everything was eerily silent.

"Be ready," Coram said, his voice hushed. "The next strike could come from anywhere."

"They are circling us," Deedubs said. "Very soon now, they're going to make their move." He turned to his son and, for the first time, Rose heard something deeper than the usual derision in his voice. "Eo, when they strike, you fight like I taught you, you hear? You forget about everything else, forget about me, forget about your fear, and you just fight. No mercy."

"'Kay, Pa. 'Kay. I will. I promise."

Footsteps. Slow. Deliberate.

"Here they come," Coram said. "For the sacrifice! For Eppersett!"

Weapons raised, everyone turned toward the sound. Rose gripped the branches, bracing herself for what was to come. Within her chest, the beating of her heart sounded like a war drum.

A ghastly figure appeared from behind the pillars, and a

gasp ran through the group. It was Meadowrue. She was in terrible shape—her face puffy and marked, blood running down her arms, a large gash on her shoulder and across her back, all of it mixed with sand. Her clothes were torn, and her swords were covered in a thick black sludge, as were the heels of her boots.

With a sly grin, she looked at each of them and shook the blood and sand out of her hair. "Guys," she said, "this is going to be fun—and a little bit brutal."

And as if on cue, the monsters attacked.

Screaming, they charged out from behind Meadowrue—a wave of white. Their surge was almost blinding, and as they descended upon the group, Rose noticed they were all different shapes and sizes. Some walked on four legs, some on two. Some looked eerily human and some like animals—outlines of them, filling the spaces of such things. But within, they all displayed deep pockets of darkness every time they shrieked or bled or gazed hungrily at their prey.

The dragons had already swooped down and begun to pick at Meadowrue's first kill, to which she quickly added a few more. She fought with a flat, stoic face, her mouth nothing but a line, as she hacked away. Beside her, Coram was just the opposite. Graceful, with no wasted movements. When he attacked, he hit, never missing. Eo, however, was obviously trapped deep in his head. He picked his spots carefully, and they were usually dodged or deflected. He was hesitant in his every move and was more on the defensive than anything else. When he saw an opening, he took it, but mostly he seemed to be protecting his father, who clearly needed no such thing. Deedubs was as ferocious as they came, more deadly than anything Rose could ever imagine. His ear was perked up, his tongue hanging far outside his mouth as if tasting the breeze for where to move next. It was quite clear his entire life had been spent in battle.

While Coram and Meadowrue had swords and the two Cobberjacks their teeth and claws, Ridge fought primarily with his fists. But what big fists they were. He swung them like anvils, crushing whatever was in his path. And if Ridge didn't get his target with his fists, his thicker branches were used like extra arms, clubbing them left and right.

As if a siren had blared, more and more dragons arrived, landing among the pillars. They weren't like the monstrous dragons Rose had always read about and imagined. These were far smaller, like the size of crocodiles, but they were as ferocious as anything she had ever seen. They were fighting over the dead, their mouths covered in the black of the satellites. Streams of fire were sprayed to keep the others from what they claimed as their own, but these blasts were erratic, often drifting out into the battle, and Rose gasped when she saw a branch of Ridge's go up in flames. She skittered down the tree and foolishly attempted to blow the fire out. *What are you doing?* she lambasted herself. *You can't even get all your birthday candles in one shot.*

Changing course, she reached out and, before the fire could spread, snapped the branch off, tossing it to the ground, where the flames quickly expired in the sand. A self-satisfied smile broke out across her face until a satellite sprung into the branches. She screamed and kicked her feet at it and, hearing her, Ridge reached up, grabbed hold of a leg, and swung the creature like a discus. Flying through the air, it crashed into a pillar and Rose watched as the stone structure began to wobble just beside Coram, who was fighting off two more satellites in its shadow. *It's going to go over*, she thought. "Coram!" He looked up just in time to see it falling, and dived out of the way. It landed with a thud right atop the two satellites, crushing the life out of them. The Stylite who had been sitting atop it went tumbling.

More and more, the satellites were coming for Ridge and Rose. They kept leaping into the tree, and Rose would cower and kick to keep them off. Ridge, however, was clearly growing weary from the relentless attacks.

Two creatures leapt for him at once and were able to knock

him to the ground as if they had taken an ax to his trunk. He crashed hard, and Rose tumbled from his branches, hitting her head against a pillar. She lay on the ground, dazed, and the two creatures, ignoring the vulnerable Ridge, glared at her instead. Their mouths opened wide, and then they charged.

In a desperate effort, Ridge managed to reach out, grabbing one by the leg and pulling it in so that his branches could finish it off. But Rose saw her death in the other's eyes. She saw it so clearly. And it made her think how much she had wasted. How she let life feed off her instead of feeding off it.

You're not ready to die, Rose. You're not.

As the creature leapt for her, its dark mouth open, she turned her head and held up her hands, her voice releasing a sharp scream.

It was all a reflex, a defensive act. But as she did so, she felt something course through her body. Something strange but very powerful, as if her voice were taking a physical shape within her. She felt like she was on fire, and there was a crackling throughout her body that converged in her hands. Opening her eyes, she watched in shock as, in midair, the creature exploded, black sludge flying everywhere.

Rose crumbled backward, her mouth hanging wide open. "I . . . I . . ."

In the dust of the battle, the group stared at one another, sharing her disbelief.

What was that? What was that? Rose, what is happening to you?

From above, the Stylite once again made his statement, one that rang out like a bell. "She is not what you think."

Chapter 9
THE UNWONTED

W hat just happened?" Rose asked, her voice twisted up inside her like barbwire. "What did I just do?"

"We were going to ask you the same thing," Meadowrue said, cleaning her swords against her pants.

Although her skin slowly recovered from paling completely white, Rose's chest continued to heave and her hands continued to tremble. Sitting on the ground, unable to move, she dazedly took in all the carnage around her—the dragons feasting on the satellites, the fallen and cracked pillars, the toppled and distraught Stylite. But most of all she focused on the dark splatter that was the creature who had leapt for her. She had done that, and she alone.

"I don't know what I did," she cried. "I . . . I just didn't want to die. That thing was coming for me and I wanted it gone. That's all. I didn't mean to do that. Honest."

"It was magic," Coram said, his voice hushed in awe. "The kind that doesn't exist in Eppersett." His breaths were deeper now, as if he were trying to completely empty his lungs. "Human magic . . . it does something to us, to our insides, that no other magic can replicate. Our world has no resistance to it. There's no defending such power."

Off to the side, Deedubs grunted and turned away. "Human magic. Hmmpf."

"You know what this means," Coram insisted. "You all do. You heard the Stylite."

Everyone was staring at Rose in a mixture of awe and deep curiosity. She shriveled up beneath their gaze, feeling as exposed as she had ever been. "It wasn't magic," she squeaked.

"Then what was it?" Meadowrue asked.

Rose hesitated. Her mouth opened and closed but nothing came out. Finally, as her face reddened more and more, her arms raised in exasperation. "Spontaneous combustion? Maybe?"

Everyone waved her off.

"When you screamed," Coram said, "something came from your hands."

"Humans don't have magic," she said.

"You're right," Deedubs said. "So then, how do you explain it?"

"I . . . I can't."

The group devolved into bickering, the meditating Stylites and the feasting dragons paying them no mind and vice versa. Above, the sun was in its descent, casting the sky in a superb mixture of reds and yellows. The winds increased, blowing sand all over, the temperature dropping rapidly.

"Um, maybe she's something even more special and stuft," Eo said.

"More special than the sacrifice?" Deedubs said in disgust to his son.

"I don't know, Pa. You know the stories . . ."

"Get that foolishness out of your head! She's just a girl, far from home. The perfect sacrifice. The Abomination will feed once again, and we'll have peace until it awakens once more. Then we'll do it all over again."

With his head lowered, Eo said, "It called her Unwonted. What's that mean?"

"It means she's unusual," Coram said, his voice distant.

Ridge pointed at Rose, shouting, "That's right! It said she isn't what we think she is!"

"So it's true, then," Meadowrue said.

Rose always hated when other people spoke about her when she was sitting right there, near but so far. "What's true?"

Coram exhaled and addressed the group, but mostly he kept his eyes on Rose. "Every so often a human enters our world. Sometimes they help us fight our enemies, displaying amazing abilities and hidden strengths, and sometimes they are weaklings and cowards and are sacrificed to the Abomination or some other monster. But every now and then, one human comes along that is not like the others. These humans are said to exist between worlds. At least their souls do. They may have been physically born in another place, but their souls have two homes. Having been torn apart, these humans don't feel whole anymore. They are constantly searching, trying to find themselves. They have the magic of Eppersett within them. And this turns them into something truly special indeed. It gives them a magic that is more powerful than anything we have here, a magic of two worlds. And it is in you, Rose Coffin."

Rose felt queasy. "What are you saying?"

"I'm saying that you can defeat the Abomination. Not for ten years, but for good. You're not just a sacrifice anymore. You're the one we've been waiting for. The one we thought would never come."

"So . . ." Rose was all too aware of how the focus on her had changed. Everyone's eyes widened; it was like they were hypnotized by her, and the feeling made her skin scrawl. To be ignored was painful, but to be singled out was unbearable.

She could hardly bring her words forward. "So, I'm . . . I'm not going to be sacrificed, then?"

"Of course you're going to be sacrificed!" Ridge said. "The legend clearly states that the Abomination will sense your magic, if it has not already done so! But before it feasts on you, it must be primed for death!"

"The three fabled weapons," Meadowrue said, practically giddy.

"Only three weapons in all the world can make the Abomination susceptible to Rose's attack, and all three must be used in unison," Coram explained. "The spiked armor of Syedel. The sword of Tarr. And the arrows of Millenten. Each lies with their fallen master. Together, they will make the Abomination vulnerable to Rose's magic. Only then can she finish this."

"Yes!" Ridge cried, clearly excited by the legend. He lifted Rose up with his branches and brought her before his eyes. "When the Abomination's great maw opens in agony from the three weapons, you must enter of your own accord! Then, and only then, in the belly of the beast, you will explode in the most incredible display of magic anyone will ever witness! Oh, I can't wait!"

Rose went limp with dread and was placed back atop Ridge. Below, everyone talked over one another in electrified tones. Rose, however, was busy replaying one specific aspect of the legend over and over in her head.

"Are we sure?" Meadowrue said. "This will really end it? The Abomination will never return?"

"Never!" Coram insisted, his hands in fists.

"Then we must set out at once!" Ridge declared.

From up in the tree, they heard a sound. A sound that confused them all. Rose, head bowed, hair in her face, was laughing.

"What's so funny?" Coram asked, eyebrows raised.

Everyone glanced back and forth at one another. Rose couldn't stop laughing. It just tumbled out of her; she had no control over it. It grew louder and louder and louder. And though everyone stared at her like she was crazy, she didn't care. It felt good. It actually felt good.

"What's so funny?" Coram asked again, clearly irritated.

She gazed down at them, their mouths all agape—only Eo had a grin, as if he understood exactly how she felt. How could they not see the irony of it all? Finally, Rose calmed down enough to say, "The legend said I have to be willing to do this. Willing! You need me to work with you. You need me to sacrifice myself and use this power."

"Yes, and . . . ?" Coram didn't see the issue.

Rose shook her head in disbelief. "There's no way that's happening, you dolt! You've been marching me along to my death since I got here. Nobody's cared about what I've had to say about any of it, how I feel, what I might be thinking. We were going to get there and you were just going to throw me at this monster and now you expect me to help you? Out of the kindness of my heart or something? No way. Forget it."

They all looked at one another, the reality sinking in. Rose could see their bodies deflate, their eyes go dark.

Coram said, "Rose, the greater good . . ."

"N-O."

"But . . . without you . . ."

"Oh, well."

Without saying a word, Deedubs padded behind a pillar. What started as a low growl became a ground-rattling roar of frustration that could be heard for miles, even sending several of the dragons to the sky in retreat.

When he returned, Deedubs, full of bitterness and through gritted teeth, said, "This opportunity may not come again for centuries. We have to take her to the queen. She'll know what to do."

"Yes," Coram said, nodding. "If anyone can convince Rose of what must be done, it will be her. She has never been denied."

There's always a first time, Rose thought. Still, she was confused and weak with fear. Something weird was going on with her body. It was cracking her open from within. And now, on top of that, there was all this talk of legends and special weapons.

"You're stronger than you think," Coram said. "Stronger than we all thought."

Rose looked up. "Yeah, well, not enough to get me out of this mess."

Minutes later, they were headed east from the pillars in search of the queen. Momentary relief had washed over Rose as her feeding to the Abomination was put on hold. For now she had the upper hand. But something told her that wasn't going to last for very long.

CHAPTER 10
TROUBLES WITH SLEEP

The desert was now well behind them, and although the wind still blew, at least it wasn't carrying sand. As they trudged through the dusk, they pulled their coats tight around them.

Coram paused, scanning the horizon. It still seemed like they had a long way to go. "It's getting late," he said, the wind blowing his hair in his face. "Let's set up camp."

As the others began preparing the fire and provisions, Coram jumped into the branches with Rose, easily pulling himself up bough by bough until he was sitting beside her. Rose shifted as far away as she could, but any more and the branch would probably snap.

She wanted to push him off—maybe he'd land on his sword or something, break a leg. Maybe she could conjure some of that magic from before, or whatever it was, if it was even anything at all. But she thought better of this and decided to just bide her time instead. When they all slept, she'd be gone.

"Everything is at stake for us," Coram said, his legs dangling but still—Rose, on the other hand, couldn't keep hers from swaying. From a distance, they probably looked like two ordinary kids sitting on the bough of a tree.

Coram sighed an especially long sigh. "We've been fighting this battle for so long nobody can remember a time before the Abomination. Eppersett used to be so much bigger then, but every time it reappears, we keep losing land that will never come back. Much of the territory south of the Zo River has become a wasteland. During the years of its slumber, we try to heal the land, we try to grow crops and repopulate it, but nothing ever takes. It's a disease, one that can't be healed. There have always been great dangers in Eppersett—no one has ever known it to be any different—but there's never been anything like this."

Rose had had enough. Still looking off, she said, "So, there's always been monsters, is that it? Not just the Abomination, but hundreds in between. So even once it's gone, something else will take its place. And then something after that, and after that. We die and for what? When does it end?"

Coram glanced down below them. "I don't know."

Rose's voice picked up steam, the words rattling off her tongue in a melodic barrage. "Where I come from, there aren't any monsters or abominations, not like the kind here anyway, but our horrors keep coming too. One thing after another. Sometimes . . . sometimes it just becomes too much. It takes everything from you. Everything. Any happiness you might have. Even the slightest bit; it's just snatched away, over and over again, until you're . . . blank. Empty. I never thought—"

Rose felt a crackling throughout her body, similar to when she was attacked among the Stylites. Her hands buzzed as if pricked with a thousand needles. The heat inside her intensified. She closed her mouth, swallowing the words that had gathered in her throat.

Coram nodded. "I've never fit in well here, Rose. I guess . . . maybe . . . It sounds like I'm a lot like you, believe it or not."

Rose rolled her eyes.

"My whole kind is—all eleven of us. Though there could be less by now—I haven't seen one in years, and the way we're hunted I don't know if I ever will. It's hard for me to see the beauty in the world that everyone else sees, though I know they see it. When the dangers are gone—that brief moment of time before the next one arrives—I see the joy. I see the peace and love in Eppersett, the bonds among the people. But I always feel the same. I want their joy. I want that life. But even though it never comes, I still fight. For them. For happiness. For love. We all do. I just . . . I just hope to one day . . . maybe . . ." He trailed off. "Do you understand?"

Rose finally turned and looked at him, if only for a second before her eyes dropped. She did understand. There has always been a yearning for happiness in her that had never been fulfilled either. "You can run," Rose said, her voice floating like a bubble. "You can find a place that isn't like this. A place where you belong."

He nodded. "I thought that too. But every place is like this, Rose. You can't escape it. You have to fight."

"Or you succumb," Rose finished. Their gazes found each other, and Rose turned away so quickly she would have fallen off the branch had he not grabbed her. All the people she had always been told to relate to, whether they were on TV or in her school, never spoke to her inner thoughts the way he just did. *A shame he wants to see you dead.*

It was very late and everyone was sleeping but them, Ridge's breaths giving the branches a gentle shake, like the perfect breeze. But she knew, if she were ever going to escape, it had to be at night when everyone slept. Unfortunately,

Coram seemed nowhere near tired. "Aren't you going to sleep?" she asked him.

He looked at her as if surprised she hadn't drifted off herself by now. "I don't sleep," he said.

Rose swallowed, her hopes going down hard. "What do you mean? Everyone sleeps."

"Maybe where you come from. But here, if someone has gold skin, it means they don't."

"How is that possible?"

"The sun. It charges us. Keeps us going through the night."

"So, you're like a walking solar panel."

"I have no idea what that is."

"You catch all the heat inside you. That's why you feel like you're on fire."

He placed a hand against his chest. "Sometimes it almost becomes too much. I have to keep blowing it free, especially during the day, or . . ." His voice drifted off.

There was some rustling below, and Rose noticed Meadowrue was thrashing in her sleep. She almost looked as if she were being attacked. Deep and chilling moans stretched out into the night. "No," she called out. "No." Hands on her head, she rocked back and forth, perilously close to the fire. "No."

Her face was illuminated by the flames, and Rose noticed something moving in Meadowrue's right ear. The cartilage began to wiggle and swell. Slowly, the ear expanded, and Meadowrue cried out even louder, curdling Rose's blood. Eo motioned to get up, but Deedubs pulled him back down. Finally, once her ear fully blossomed, a ball fell out and rolled near the fire. Meadowrue, pale and shaking, woke up. She looked around and caught Coram and Rose staring while the others slept, or pretended to. Nobody said a word. Meadowrue just dusted herself off, picked up the red orb, and hurried out into the night.

"Is . . . is she okay?" Rose asked.

Coram shook his head. "Nothing about Meadowrue is okay."

"Where is she going?"

"The Cemetery of Bad Dreams."

"You're going to have to explain that one to me," Rose said.

"Just thinking about the place is enough to make even my body go cold. It's dark and haunted grounds."

Rose's thoughts were racing, her voice gaining in pitch. "But why is she going? What the heck was that red thing? Why'd she bring it with her? Why is everyone acting like this is normal?"

"Because it is. When nightmares are born, they hatch from red orbs within your head. Before they can crack and escape, they must be buried so that they can no longer threaten you or this world. That is where she is going. Most people here have evolved past dreams. Either that or they have trained themselves to have very few and, thus, very few nightmares. Meadowrue, however, never seemed to get that far. She has more restless nights than anyone I know."

"What about you?" Rose asked.

"I don't sleep. That means I don't dream." He paused, looking away. When he spoke again, his voice was weak. "And that means no nightmares."

Rose wondered if this was a fair trade or not. "It must be hard for her," she said, gazing into the darkness in which Meadowrue disappeared. "To find some happiness. Some ordinary kind of happiness."

"There's nothing ordinary about happiness, Rose. Happiness is as special as things get."

CHAPTER 11
SUMMERCRESS CASTLE

The Order walked on in silence. In a very short time, things had gotten much more complicated. The Abomination could now be killed, but first they would have to recover three magical weapons that were spread out all across Eppersett and very well guarded. They also had to hope the queen could convince Rose to sacrifice herself—which Rose had to admit was never going to happen—and even if she could be convinced, Rose would still have to learn how to master her abilities in a rather short time. Meadowrue was dealing with her constant nightmares and demons, Deedubs continued to belittle Eo, Coram was breathing heavier and heavier, and even Ridge began to lose his good cheer. No, things were as bleak as ever.

Still, there were enough strange sights along the miles of land over the next two days to keep their thoughts from dwelling on such things. Grazing fields of three-foot-high blue grass were hairy apelike beasts full of muscle called Jarries, and they had huge antlers, bushy tails, and violet bodies. Riding them, with sharp pronged rods at their sides, were sickly-looking gray creatures who kept leaning their oversized heads back and crying out, signaling to the other riders around them as they harvested the crops with long arms that reached all the way to the ground. These gangly things were Saddats, and according to Coram, they supplied Eppersett with a majority of its food, a crop called life grass and one of the only things Rose would eat.

At dusk on the second day since vacating the Stylites, they found a pair of parallel tracks and followed them east, walking in the wide space between them, the grass as tall as their knees and the bugs as big as their fists. To Rose, the tracks looked like they ran twin trains. They twisted off in either direction, but appeared very old. It was decided then that the group would camp there for the night, beside the tracks.

Rose, once again, had no chance of escaping, Coram keeping his eyes locked on her at all times. But she felt more and more confident that she might be able to find a way home. After all, she was useless to them now. There was no way she was going to sacrifice herself for them, not ever, and there was no way they could make her.

"You know," Coram said, as if reading her mind. "If you don't cooperate, we could still just sacrifice you. We'd at least get ten years of peace. That's better than nothing." He leaned back and locked his hands behind his head, a sly grin on his face. All Rose could do was fold her arms and turn away from him, stewing in her anger.

In the morning—a sunrise so bright there could have been two suns in the sky—Rose woke and was facing something so massive and strange that she knew it hadn't been there the night before. It couldn't have been. Sitting on the tracks, about a quarter of a mile away, was a huge castle.

It was a monstrous structure, broad and tall, with five imposing towers, at the top of which flew purple flags emblazoned with a dark square with three circles within it, one inside the other. To Rose it was a troublesome eye that remained fixed on her every move. From the center of the castle rose the keep like a stone serpent from the coldest depths. The windows, save for the highest ones, were all bricked up, and numerous guards were on the lookout along the parapets and in the turrets, arrows at the ready. It appeared as if the castle had sustained major damage over the years; its moss-covered walls were battered, the stone in pieces, the towers ready to fall.

"Summercress Castle," Coram announced, still with pride. "I admit, it has seen better days."

"And it will again!" Ridge added. "Won't it, Rose? You'll see to that!"

Rose, however, just continued to stare at the awesome sight, her brow scrunched in confusion. "How . . . Where did it . . . I don't understand . . . Do you have engines here? You have that kind of technology?"

Ridge scratched the side of his head. "I don't know what an engine is, but we don't need it! We have Sorums!"

"And what's a Sorum?"

Ridge glanced at Coram. "She has a lot to learn, this one! Has no clue about Sorums! I thought everyone knew about those buggers!"

Coram caught Rose's gaze and nodded his head toward the castle. "Have you ever met a queen, Rose?"

"Back home? All the time," she answered, her eyes locked on the highest tower.

"Oh." Coram's shoulders slumped; he kicked at the ground. "Well, you're going to meet another."

Circling around the front of the castle in an attempt to locate the drawbridge, Rose noticed how the entire structure looked as if it had been ripped from the ground and placed high on a stone platform. In the darkness beneath were scores of large, rusty wheels, though Rose saw no motor or gears to move them. On their trip toward the entrance, they had to walk over huge, thick chains that hung from the base and snaked their way into the distance. In fact, it wasn't so much walking over them as it was scaling the metal—each link was bigger than Rose was.

Almost a half hour later, when they finally found the drawbridge and waited for it to lower, Rose craned her neck, taking in the castle in full. Up close it was even more impressive, more imposing, and very, very cold in its shadow. Suddenly, she felt the chilling and full weight of meeting a queen, and thought the pressure might send her straight through the earth. Never in her life did she imagine she'd be important enough to stand before royalty.

Lowered, the drawbridge was more like a steep ramp than an overpass. They scaled it, but the metal gate beyond would not rise. To their right, a man with a face so green it was as if he were deeply sick sat looking out a small window at them. He said the queen hadn't seen any visitors in quite some time and that that wasn't about to change. He suggested they go home.

"There have been several attempts on Queen Sequoia's life lately," the gatekeeper added when Coram insisted how important their visit was. "Not to mention what has happened to her son. And there's no way I'm going to be responsible for another attack. Leave now."

With a huff, Rose sat back in the branches. She hadn't slept well since she came here. The food made her ill, and she was badly homesick. The sun was now bearing down on her with a brutal force. She was sweating uncontrollably, she was thirsty, sunburned, had a rash on her arm, and Deedubs wouldn't stop growling and pacing, his long nails clicking on the wood like the loudest of clocks. The arguing with the gatekeeper grew louder and louder and louder.

Finally, Rose couldn't take it anymore. She stood up in the tree, balled her fists, and screamed.

A static charge ran through her body like a bolt of lightning, buzzing her hands as if they were set on fire. A blast came from them, burning a branch in the tree and part of her sleeve before exploding against the gate. She fell back against the bough, staring at her hands, her jaw hanging open, a smoking hole in their path.

In confusion, she glanced up at the gatekeeper, who was still in his window, a look of shock on his face that she was sure matched her own.

The group, however, didn't have time to be dumbfounded. Seizing their opportunity, they moved through the blasted gate and into the castle.

Just as they crossed the threshold, the gatekeeper reached them, nearly tripping down the stairs. Struggling for oxygen, he held out his hand and ordered them to stop.

"We must see the queen," Coram reiterated.

"No!" the gatekeeper shouted, attempting to shove them back out, his eyes crazed. "Get out of here! Get out! It'll be my head!"

But Ridge merely picked him up and moved him aside, patting his head as he went past.

"Guards!" the gatekeeper yelled. "Guards!" But there was no need to scream; they had come running the moment they had heard the explosion.

Rose glanced around. All eyes were on them now. The guards were assembling in massive numbers, heading down from their towers while others were pouring out of the armory, blades glistening. They were as large as bears on their back legs with glowing orange eyes peering out from the darkness beneath their helmets. They had swords and spears and maces and axes, and they chanted in a strange language as they charged.

"Hurry," Coram said. "To the queen!"

"And where's that?" Meadowrue asked, swords in hand. To Rose, she looked like she would rather stay behind and fight.

"I don't know," Coram said. "This way," and he took off

deeper into the castle, practically dragging Meadowrue behind him.

Arrows rained down on the group, one sailing just past Rose's head and sticking into one of Ridge's branches. He didn't seem fazed by it at all, though when Rose yanked it free, he gave a soft little whimper as brownish-red sap dripped from the wound.

The guards chased the group through an empty chapel and across a vast kitchen. What looked like a boar in an apron stood cooking over a fire, yelling at them to get out of her kitchen.

"Where are we going?" Meadowrue shouted.

Coram was breathing heavily, carefully expelling his rising heat. "I don't know!"

"Step aside," Deedubs said with a growl. "Let us lead the way!"

Eo pulled his father to the front, the two of them using their noses to find the queen.

"Um, this way, I think. Pretty sure."

"It's our lives, boy!" Deedubs shouted. "Our lives! Be positive!"

"I am! I'm positive, Pa! This way!"

They entered the great hall. A staircase was at the far end. "There!" Eo yelled. They hurried for it, but before they were even halfway across the room, their path was cut off by at least fifty guards. The Order stopped and turned around, but found the rest of the guards had caught up with them.

"Surrounded," Meadowrue said, almost with pleasure. "Looks like we're going to make a stand after all."

Deedubs's blank eyes found his son. "You failed us, boy. We were counting on you!"

Eo sniffed the air ahead. "She's just past there, Pa. I know it. If we had a little more time . . ."

"Excuses! A warrior doesn't have excuses!"

"Maybe I'm not—"

"Enough! It's time for battle. Pray you survive."

"There's too many," Coram said. "We'll never make it."

Deedubs snorted at this. "Cowards, all of you. I will do it myself."

As the guards warily closed in, Rose's chest tightened with fear. Her frantic thoughts kept racing back to what she did at the gate and in the Field of Stylites. *Maybe you could do the same here*, she thought. *Okay, but how did you do it, exactly?* She held out her hands, extending them toward the guards, but nothing happened. She wasn't even sure what she wanted to happen. Kill them? Maybe she could make them disappear? Was that even possible? She closed her eyes and waved her hands. Nothing. She pulled them back and then shot them forward. *Rose, you look like a child playing pretend.*

Coram held his sword in both hands. "Protect Rose. She's all that matters."

The lead guard held up his hand, barking orders. When it dropped, they would charge.

Rose was covered in panic, a thick coat of it. She trembled everywhere, her heart rolling all the way up into her throat. She thought of her parents, her brother, and how she'd never see them again. The pain was overwhelming.

Then came that same sensation, clearing out the pain and panic. Her hands vibrated and her body warmed. *It's happening*, she thought.

But what exactly was happening she had no clue. The feeling just continued to intensify without any results. Something built in her, but there was no release.

Across the room, the lead guard's arm dropped. A shout went out, and the guards charged, some of them dropping to four legs as they stampeded forward. Rose knew that whatever was going to come had to come now.

Please. Hurry.

But nothing happened. She felt herself overheating, her temperature incredibly high. Sweat built up all across her body. Her head throbbed.

"Ready," Coram said to the others. "We fight as one."

"Ah, I've been starving for battle," Deedubs said. "Summercress Castle is a fine place to die."

They'll never win, Rose. You're never going to get a chance to escape if you don't do something right now. They're going to kill you. All of you.

Strangely, the buzzing in her hands began to fade. *No. No! What's happening? Why isn't it working?*

The guards were nearly upon them now, their weapons raised, their shouts filling the hall. Coram and the others let loose their own battle cries as Rose braced herself.

"Stoooooppp!"

As if slamming into an invisible wall, the guards came to a grinding halt. Immediately, they dropped to their knees, their heads bowed, their bodies quivering.

Rose turned around knowing who she would see, though nothing could prepare her for the sight. Queen Sequoia stood at the foot of the staircase, as terrifying a presence as Rose had ever witnessed.

CHAPTER 12
QUEEN SEQUOIA

The queen had no face. There were no eyes, no ears, no mouth, no nose. Only flesh. Pale, vein-filled flesh that pulsed and throbbed as if something were living underneath. And when she spoke her voice emanated from above, as if from a thundercloud.

"There's magic here," she said in a hollow voice, which echoed and cracked in the ears of everyone. "Very rare magic. That of a human."

She stood completely still, her hands folded delicately at her waist. She wore a spectral dress that flared out around her feet like a pool of water. It clung to her skeletal frame, the collar high and pointed, sharp as knives. Atop her head was not a crown, but a wreath of dead flowers.

There was a palpable tension in the room. Rose could hear the guards trembling within their armor. Even the birds in Ridge's branches hid their faces in their feathers. All around them, it felt as if the walls had been pulled in.

Although Queen Sequoia didn't have eyes, it was clear she was looking over the group very carefully, and it was especially evident when she settled on Rose. "You," she said in a lightning strike of a voice.

Rose nearly fainted in the branches, her body icing over and freezing her in a position that was as gnarled as the tree. "M-me?" she said, her voice cracking. It was like being called on in the middle of an assembly, the entire school there, and Rose stood, only to realize she was naked.

"You!" The queen's hand raised, a finger pointing straight at her. Her fingers were twice as long as they should have been and with no nails at the tips, though they still came to a sharp point. "It was your magic I sensed. Outside the castle and within these walls. Human magic."

"No. I . . . I don't know what . . . I tried, but . . ."

"Speak up!" She stepped closer, her chin raised as if sniffing the air. "Fear. Cowardice. How is it I sense such weakness in you? Tell me, how can someone with abilities such as yours be so fearful?"

Rose had no response; she just lowered her head and averted her eyes. This was just who she was. She never imagined there was anything else to be.

"You may have managed to survive in your world, girl, but you won't here," the queen said. "In Eppersett, such insecurities will bring you to your fate soon enough. One way or another."

Coram, his eyes on the floor, cleared his throat and said, "She's the one, Your Highness. The Unwonted. There is no doubt. But she refuses to cooperate. That is why we sought you out. We know your time is precious and that these days have been most difficult for you, but we hoped you would know what to do. We hoped you would be able to convince her."

The queen was silent for a moment. "The sacrifice of sacrifices. The one whose death will end it all. And yet she refuses?"

After another silence, this one much longer, Queen Sequoia turned back to her guards and waved her arms. "Clear out! Now! Leave me with my guests."

Everyone dispersed—practically running over one another to get out of the hall—and the queen snapped her long fingers, creating a loud pop that stuck in the ears. A chair was immediately brought out from a side room by two piggish servants and placed before her. She took a seat, her dress running like rain against her legs, her posture stiff and perfect.

No one knew what to do or how to behave. There were a lot of nervous looks and this made Rose even more frightened.

"This time is different than the others," Queen Sequoia said. "The Abomination has grown too powerful too quickly. It will no longer rest, not even with a hundred sacrifices. There will be no slowing it down, no time to rebuild what has been destroyed. It dies, or we die."

"Your Highness," Deedubs said. "Forgive me, but how can you know such a thing? This girl is a coward. Like them all. That's why she came here. She will never be brave enough for the task. We must sacrifice her ourselves and hope for a future with a more heroic human."

"You're not forgiven, Deedubs," Queen Sequoia snapped. "Don't you dare ever question my knowledge!"

Rose was shocked to see the Cobberjack recoil in fear and shame. But there was no mistaking it; even if Rose wished to help, she would never have the strength to do so.

"He's right," Rose said. "I'm no fighter. I run. That's what I do. I don't want any of this. I just want to go home. Now."

As she said these words, she was surprised at how true they were. Home had always been a place to flee—she was like her father in that way—but this world was no escape. It wasn't freedom and it wasn't safety. It was dangerous. Deadly. Back home she had a fighting chance, but here . . . it was hopeless.

"Home?" the queen shouted, rising from her chair. "Home? Girls like you have no home! Otherwise you'd never wind up here in the first place!"

Rose was overwhelmed with emotion, her eyes aching as much as her heart. "That's not true! I have a home! I do!"

"Home is not merely where one lays her head, little Rose. A home is something you help create. A home is a place you fight for, a place—no matter the difficulties—you never abandon, because it is built on happiness, on love, on hope. And we are losing ours. But you . . . you can change that."

Rose shook her head. "I'm not going to die for you. And I'm certainly not going to die for a world that isn't my own."

The queen slammed her hand against the chair. "Yes, you will!" Her voice rocked the castle, everyone bracing themselves. It took some moments before everything settled. "There is a glaring hole in the world you come from, Rose. And it is there because all humans are the same at the very core. The ugliness, the selfishness of each of you. So concerned with your own individual little problems that the world around you collapses and you hardly notice a thing. You are blind to the suffering of others. Blind and indifferent. The sky falls but only on you. Eppersett is different. Any one of us would gladly sacrifice ourselves to the Abomination if it meant its certain destruction. We would never stand by while millions die all around us. Not like you humans. Here, we stand together."

Everyone turned and looked at Rose as she sunk down in the branches. She never asked for this. Any of it. She just wanted to get away. From SallyAnn, from school, from her parents, her brother, her struggles. From life. "I don't know what you expect from me. I'm just a kid."

"I expect you to die," Queen Sequoia said. "I expect you to give yourself up for the greater good. Become the hero you were meant to be. You are a girl of rare magic, Rose. A weapon to rid us of the Abomination once and for all."

Rose, chin quivering, shook her head. "I won't do it."

The queen took a step toward her, and every ounce of Rose's body wanted to back away. It was telling her to climb higher in the branches or jump down and take off running, never looking back. But she didn't. She held her ground.

Slowly, the queen neared, extending her hand. "Come. Walk with me."

Rose hesitated, staring at the claw that seemed to extend and extend and extend toward her. It reached far up into the branches, until it was no more than a foot from her face.

"Come," Queen Sequoia repeated, and the tone was soft, as if it were somehow in Rose's head and in her head alone.

Gazing at the queen's blank face, Rose was struck by a hazy memory. She couldn't remember what exactly, just the feeling. Like she was a young child again and staring at her mother.

Rose reached out and took her hand, the long fingers wrapping around hers, not with force and pressure, but gently.

She was led down from Ridge's branches, away from the group and up the main staircase. As she went, she glanced back at Coram and the others, her eyes wide and full of fear and confusion. Coram nodded at her, and she knew it was his way of saying she would be okay, though she hardly believed him.

Rose and the queen walked in silence. They were still holding hands, though Rose had tried to pull hers away several times. The queen only held it with the tips of her fingers, but the grip was powerful nonetheless.

Without turning toward her, Queen Sequoia asked, "What do you see, Rose? What do you see when you look at me?"

Rose felt her throat ice up. "Nothing."

The queen nodded very subtly. "Interesting."

They reached the top of the stairs, their bodies illuminated by dozens of massive candles lining the walls, the wax dripping down and across the floor creating a strange patchwork. Farther along, the queen pushed open a wooden door that creaked like an old tree in a storm. Inside was what must have been her chambers. It was an extravagant room, full of bizarre and interesting objects that glittered and shined, but

Rose could only focus on the large four-poster bed in the center, and the figure lying upon it. Hundreds of dead flowers covered the body—roses, to be exact. They were all around the bed, on the floor, on the pillows, hanging in the snow-white canopy. A smell lingered in the air, a stale bitterness, like acid in the nose. It was enough to make Rose's eyes water.

The queen made her way toward the bed, and Rose's pace slowed as her heart plunged straight to her knees. The air had left the room the moment she entered, and she was now having trouble breathing. Her body tingled, not with magic, but with the absence of it. This had happened before. She had felt exactly like this some time ago, but in her terror, she couldn't place it.

"Come," Queen Sequoia said, glancing back at her. "You need to see this."

No, you don't, Rose thought. *Whatever's on that bed is the last thing you need to see. Just run. Get out of here and never come back.*

But she didn't run. As if in a trance, she was pulled forward. Or was the bed coming to her? Everything slowed down. She could hear her heart; she could see the dust floating in the sunlit air. Something in the room chirped steadily, a sound that pounded deep within her ears.

Whoever was on the bed wasn't moving, hadn't since she first walked in.

Please don't let him be dead, she thought. *Please don't.*

When she had finally reached the bed—after what felt like an hour—the queen raised her hand and slowly moved aside the curtain, revealing the body within. Rose wanted to shut her eyes but it was as if they were stapled open. Peering in, she gazed upon the body, and a horrid scream barreled its way up her throat when she realized it was her brother. She spun away from the bed, stifling the scream with her hand, her eyes slamming closed as the tears built steadily behind them.

Breathe, Rose. Breathe. It's not him. It can't be.

"Look again," said the queen.

One eye opened, then the other. When Rose finally glanced back, she didn't see her brother anymore, just another blank face to match the queen's.

"Tell me, Rose, what did you see when you looked upon him?" Queen Sequoia asked.

Rose was slow to respond; her entire body was still trembling. The color of her skin had yet to return. "My . . . my brother."

The queen nodded as if she understood. "This is my son, the future king," she said. "He is linked to this land, and when it suffers, he suffers. His life has never been a pleasant one, but ever since the Abomination's latest return to Eppersett, he has suffered like never before. And now he sleeps and the

Abomination will never rest again. Even if you were to succeed in its destruction, I'm not sure if my son will ever fully recover. It is my hope that he will, but that is all it is. A hope."

There was an eerie silence, the queen's blank face remaining locked on Rose's for an agonizing length of time. "Sing to him," Queen Sequoia said.

Rose's hand lay across her heart as she backed away. "Sing? I . . . I don't understand. Why?"

"Heal him. Please." There was desperation in her voice. If she had eyes, Rose knew they would be filled with tears right now.

"I can't. My voice isn't enough."

The queen turned away, nodding. "I know." She moved over to a window and gazed out, all Eppersett laid out before her. "Tell me, why is it that you saw your brother?"

Rose was unaware she was clutching herself, the only hug she could find. She wished her mother was here; she needed her strength. "He's sick too," she said.

The queen turned back. "Will he not awaken either?"

Rose shook her head. "No."

"Have you . . . have you given up hope?"

It was now Rose's turn to cry. Her eyes watered and she stared at the floor, nodding. Her chin quivered as she tried to speak. "Y-yes."

And once it began, once she admitted she had given up on her brother, it wouldn't stop. She collapsed on the floor, weeping, and the queen came to her side. She bent down and rested her long fingers on Rose's shoulders.

"I may be able to help him, Rose. We have things here—potions, remedies, magic—that you could never imagine. Things that are sure to wake your brother from his slumber."

"You . . . you do?" Rose asked, wiping at her face.

"Yes. And if you were to help us, I would make sure our treatments reached him—magic crosses over, you know. I could do that for you. I could get it to him. A thank-you for your sacrifice."

Rose's heart smashed against her chest, and her mind flared open. In some magical future, she saw her mother standing over her brother's bed, as she did every night. But this time he opened his eyes. This time he said, "Hello. I've missed you." Rose wept just as she imagined her mother would. She wept at their embrace, at their long-awaited reunion. Her father's guilt would be washed away. Their lives could start over. She wept at her family's much-deserved happiness.

"But . . . but what if I can't do it? What if I fail? I'm not strong like Coram and Meadowrue. I'll never make it."

Rose stared deep into the queen's face now and, very slowly, an image began to form. A girl? A woman? Both? But as the features took shape across the wasteland of flesh, a loud noise erased them. The castle quaked beneath their feet, objects falling all around them, the walls crumbling, glass shattering. Outside there were screams.

The queen ran to the window, and Rose followed, twisted with dread. Gazing out, she could see there was something in the sky. Something long and white, like a plane's contrail mixing with the clouds. It must have been over three hundred feet long. It writhed in the air, heading away from them. But to her horror, she watched as it slowly turned back, looking for a second strike. It was then that she realized it was a giant snake. It was so incredibly big it was as if one snake had eaten another and then another and another, until every snake in existence was devoured, creating some monstrous nightmare. Its head was the size of her home, and it had small wings just at the end of it, as well as near the tip of its tail. "Where did that come from?" Rose asked, though she already knew the answer.

The queen's hand braced against the window. "It knows you are here, Rose. It knows what you are capable of. The Abomination has sent it to kill you."

CHAPTER 13
RUNAWAY CASTLE

As Rose watched the snake make its way back toward them—slithering across the clouds, mouth opening and closing—the castle began to shake from the other side.

Rose's head snapped in that direction, her eyes bulging. It sounded like a bomb. "What was that?"

Though her face was inscrutable, the queen's voice was clearly stricken with the same intense dread. "There are two of them." Flipping her gown so that the fabric snapped, she streaked across the room, throwing open her chamber door with barely a touch. When she spoke, her voice boomed throughout the castle, traveling down every staircase and hallway, across every ceiling and floor. "Battle stations! Every

119

hand defends the castle this day!" she cried. "Alert Spectra! Have her awaken Ramsey this instant! Get this castle moving! Now! Head for the Hollow!"

Retreating back into her chambers, she paced the room, talking quickly to herself, hands gesticulating in a desperate search for answers. "We get to the Hollow and we might be safe. They can't reach us there. But how far away is it? Twenty miles? Thirty?" She sat on the bed beside her son. Her head turned to him, and she reached out and grasped his hand. "I wish you were here," she said. "I need your strength. I put on a brave front in your absence, but I am weakening. Please, return to me."

The castle quaked again, and the queen jumped to her feet, the window filling with long-dormant dust shaken free from the beast. "We're going to have to fight," she said.

"But the Hollow . . . ?" Rose asked. She wasn't sure what the Hollow was exactly, but it sounded like a much better option than taking on two giant flying snakes.

"I'm not sure we'll make it there in one piece," Queen Sequoia answered gravely. She sat back down on the bed, seemingly stunned into silence. As the castle was struck yet again, debris falling down into the room, she grabbed the future king's hand once more.

Rose just stood there, unsure what to do. The queen had stopped moving. She didn't talk, not to her son, herself, or

Rose. It wasn't even clear she knew Rose was still there. the ceiling continued to rain down on them, the screams from outside had found their way into the room and it was as if they slapped Rose in the face, freeing her from her stupor. Without another word, she turned around and hurried downstairs and into the chaos.

Outside the tower, the castle swarmed with confusion, everyone running back and forth dodging slabs of falling stone, grabbing weapons, and hurrying for the parapets and turrets, children being escorted to the lower levels, howling with fear. *Run. Now, Rose. No one would ever notice.* And she knew it was true. She could escape the castle amidst all the confusion, ditch Coram and the others, and head for home, the threat of the Abomination left behind for good.

Go back to the woods. Go back to the place where they found you. There has to be a way back. Nodding to herself, she took three strides toward the gate, when she suddenly stopped, her feet practically sinking into the ground. The queen's promise echoed through her head like an alarm. Her brother could be saved. He could be awakened and then her parents would be saved too. It would be the best thing Rose could ever do for them, and if she left now that would all disappear.

With a scream of deep frustration, she turned around and, fists clenched, walked deeper into the fray. People crashed all sides, spinning her around several times

_mpered a bit and fell to the ground, her breath-

ying as the chaos around her mounted.

"Are you okay? I was so worried," Coram said, his face long with distress as he helped her to her feet. Rose, tears brimming in her eyes, threw her arms around him. She never thought she'd be so relieved to see his face.

When they separated, she looked him in the eye and said, "The snakes, they're here for me. This is all my fault. We have to help these people. We have to do whatever we can."

"Yes!" Ridge cried, slapping his hands together.

Deedubs let loose a howl. "Together, we will teach them the meaning of fear!"

Rose looked around and suddenly realized the whole group was together. No one had run off; no one was looking out only for themselves. They had been called upon to risk their lives for the good of the world, just like Rose, and still they remained. A strange feeling mixed in her gut. It was like a long search had finally ended. Under different circumstances, she thought she might even be happy.

Glancing at each of them, she said, "We just have to hold them off until we reach the Hollow."

"Is that where we're going? Is that what the queen said?" Coram asked as Deedubs mumbled something about cowardice.

"I think so. But why? What is it?"

Coram turned and led her and the group to the staircase that would take them to the parapets and a fight with the snakes. Meadowrue was rubbing her swords together, the sound metallic and hungry just like her eyes.

"The Hollow is a path that was cut straight through the Woodlong Mountains so that the castle could pass through," Coram explained. "It barely fits, but that's what should make it a good defense against the snakes. They would have to do a frontal assault. Concentrated. We could throw everything we have at them. A smart plan."

"That's why she's the queen!" Ridge stated.

"Will we make it?" Rose asked as they reached the top of the stairs. "I mean, we haven't even started to move yet. Are we supposed to wait for some wind or something?"

Glancing down, Rose saw the thick, heavy chains that were built into the castle walls begin to move. They lifted high off the ground—something a hundred men couldn't do—and she followed the links all the way to the front of the castle and beyond. There were four chains in all, and they were strapped to something very big. It was like a mountain rising from the ground.

Rose pushed her way past the scores of guards lining up along the parapet, arrows at the ready for the next approaching snake. Her eyes were wide as she strained for a better look at what this castle used as an engine. Rising up from its slumber, rattling the chains and shaking the ground, was a giant.

"Ramsey!" the people cried. "Ramsey!"

Rose stood slack-jawed at the awesome sight. *So, that's a Sorum*, she thought. Ramsey must have been close to a hundred feet tall, casting a long shadow over the castle, the sun a halo around his head. He was broad and round-shouldered with legs like stone pillars, and his hair was dark and greasy, hanging well past his stubbled chin and filled with earthen debris. The chains were attached to a thick leather vest he wore, on the shoulder of which Rose noticed something moving. What she first considered to be a bug turned out to be a woman. She stood in a small pocket near the back of Ramsey's neck, shouting commands into his ear. This, Rose assumed, must be Spectra, his caretaker.

Immediately, the castle lurched forward, the wheels screeching to urgent life underneath. Knowing what to expect, everyone was well braced against the walls, save for Rose and her group, who were instantly thrown about like playthings. Their heads slammed hard against the ground and walls, their bodies landing in unorthodox positions, upside down and twisted. When they managed to untangle themselves and get back to their feet, Rose noticed Deedubs was missing. Her heart sank when she realized that he must have been tossed over the parapet wall.

"Deedubs!" she shrieked, and everyone ran to the wall, searching for any sign of what might have happened to him. As they looked over the side, gasps stuck in their throats. He was fifty feet above the ground, dangling precariously by the leash between his teeth. In the far corner of the wall, Eo had somehow managed to keep the rope in his mouth, his legs braced against the stone, his entire body straining to keep his father from certain death, although he too was almost entirely over the side.

"Pa," Eo whimpered.

Ridge, who was nearest, grabbed hold of Eo, and together, they began to pull the Cobberjack to safety. Slowly, Deedubs was raised, the rope straining against the sharp edge of the stone. He was no more than three feet from the top when the castle was struck yet again, the snake slamming the wall less than twenty feet away. With the rattling tremor, Eo went fully over the side, Ridge just barely catching him by his hind legs. Meanwhile, the rope slipped from Deedubs's mouth. He held on now by nothing more than the very tips of his aged front teeth.

Coram, Meadowrue, and Rose reached the struggling trio, grabbing hold of Ridge and pulling with everything they had. "Heave!" Ridge cried. "Heave!"

Rose glanced to her left, noticing the second snake approaching fast. "It's coming," she yelled. "Another one!"

"If it hits, we're going to lose him!" Ridge said, panic in his voice.

With no other choice, Meadowrue let go of the group and pulled free her swords. Looking at her in disbelief, Rose said, "Rue, what are you doing? We need your help!"

"You're getting it." And when the snake neared, Meadowrue simply jumped over the side, fell through the air, and landed directly on its back, her two swords driving down deep into its scales. The snake writhed in pain, pulling away from the wall as it cried out.

"Now!" Ridge yelled.

Together, they pulled, all their strength channeled into each tug. A minute later, Deedubs and Eo were lifted over the wall to safety. The two Cobberjacks collapsed together, exhausted, Eo licking his father's face over and over. "I thought I lost you, Pa. I thought I lost you."

"You know I demand an honorable death, and an honorable death I will receive. No fall is going to take me."

The castle was moving quickly now. Ramsey, who had started out at a slow pace, was running full stride across Eppersett. The ride was smooth, the castle gliding over the tracks with ease, wind in everyone's hair. The walls were struck repeatedly, guards falling over the sides like leaves off a tree. The snakes had dozens of arrows in them, though they hardly slowed.

Rose watched helplessly as Meadowrue fought to hold on, her body jerked about, her legs in the air behind her, her grasp on the swords loosening.

"She needs help!" Rose cried, and when the snake was in range, Coram, with no comment or any hesitation, jumped on as well.

He landed hard, falling down the side of the beast, just barely getting a grip to keep from plunging to the ground. Steadily, he climbed up the snake's back and past Meadowrue, until he reached the beast's head. Then, raising his sword high, he brought it down right between the creature's eyes. The head went limp and the snake's wings stopped flapping as if something was severed. Suddenly, they found themselves in a lightning-fast nosedive. Rose looked on horrified as Ramsey led the castle farther into the distance, Meadowrue and Coram crashing hard to the ground behind them in a cloud of debris.

Angered at the loss of its brethren, the remaining snake picked up steam, screaming toward the castle. It swiped hard, thrashing wildly with its tail, and the castle wall looked close to collapse.

Ridge grabbed hold of Rose, shaking her. "The arrows aren't enough! We're not enough! It has to be you! Use your magic! Now!"

"But I don't know how!"

"Try! Try anything! Or all is lost! Hurry!"

He let go and Rose backed away, her eyes darting from side to side. She lowered her head and bit her lip as she tried to settle her scrambling thoughts into something logical.

You know it's tied to your voice, Rose. But it's not just that. You can't just sing or scream. It has to be directed. Aimed like a weapon or something. But how in the world do you do that?

The snake attacked again, dozens of guards falling to their deaths as the entire castle tilted, the left set of wheels rising off the tracks, then slamming back down. With her eyes focused directly on the snake, trembling and desperate, Rose shrieked, but nothing happened.

The castle continued to roar east through the territory. In the distance, the Hollow could just be made out. It wasn't very far now. But glancing at the castle's damage, Rose knew it couldn't sustain much more. If she didn't do something soon, they'd never make it.

Rose focused again, taking a deep breath. *It's up to you now, Rose. The snake has to be stopped. It has to. Forget all the eyes on you. Pretend you're alone. Pretend you're with your brother. He sees you. He sees you, Rose.* Out of the corner of her eye, she could see the snake maniacally slithering toward them. It was coming in fast, its dark mouth wide open, its wings beating viciously. *You can do it. It's now or never. Try. Do it. Do it. Do it!* DO IT!!!

Eyes closed, hands extended out before her, she opened her mouth and let loose a long ear-piercing note, nothing in her mind but the rapid destruction of the snake. As the creature bore down on the castle for one final blow, wounds began to appear all across its body. With each passing second that Rose held the note, more and more blood flowed, the snake ripping open in a million places. Shredded to pieces, it veered away from the castle and crashed straight into the ground.

A wild cheer ripped through the crowd, and everyone surrounded Rose, her body still buzzing with magic. They clutched at her and raised her up and cheered her on. And it wasn't because she was the sacrifice. It was because of what she'd done; though she was still unsure of what, exactly, that was. She was shaking all over, but relief was in the air. As was victory.

It was hers. A small smile crossed her lips. And then she fainted.

CHAPTER 14
ALONG THE RIVER ZO

The river was called the Zo and, as Ridge explained to Rose, "It's Eppersett's longest river! Can you believe it? Our longest river has the shortest name! Zo, *Z-O*! Two letters! Isn't that amazing?"

Rose raised her brows, a grunted affirmation squeezing past her tight pink lips.

Really, there were a lot of things she found amazing. This entire world for one, that her voice gave her some kind of power here for another, that she had just brought down a giant monster snake all by herself, that they were able to find Coram and Meadowrue five miles from the castle and in one piece, as well as about, oh, three million other things including, most miraculously, that she might actually have a chance to save her brother. But a long river with two letters? No. She didn't find that amazing. At all.

Thankfully her fainting spell back at the castle didn't last very long, but it was enough to let her know that she had expelled far too much energy in one attack. If she wanted to make sure she saw this through to its proper conclusion, fulfilling her end of the bargain, she'd have to be careful from here on out. At least that was what the queen had told her after she came to. If she was ever going to reach the Abomination, she would have to gain better control of her voice.

They followed the Zo River south. At some point on their journey, they were supposed to reach Lemonwyll Bridge, which was so long and so wide an entire city was built across it. This was their destination, their first stop on the way to the Abomination. According to Coram, the bridge was almost as old as Eppersett itself. It had its own castle, its own king and queen, its own army and laws, most of them very loose. "It's a rowdy place," Coram explained, "full of incorrigible monsters, but don't concern yourself with it too much. Our sole purpose for being there is the labyrinth in the center of the bridge, hidden just below the castle. That's where we'll find our first weapon in bringing down the Abomination."

"The armor?" Rose asked.

"The armor of Syedel!" Ridge clarified. "The warlock deserves our respect!"

"Spiked armor, you imbecile," Meadowrue said with a snap. "If you really mean to show respect."

The group was tense since they had departed for this new phase of their mission. Coram was breathing heavier, Meadowrue kept clutching at her throat as if her head were about to separate from it, Ridge's branches shook without any wind, and Eo was whimpering. The only one it didn't seem to affect was Deedubs.

Large ships sailed up and down the Zo River, though the majority of them kept very close to the west bank rather than the east. It was as if there was an imaginary line dividing the river and all the boats made sure to keep on the same side. Something told Rose this was for a very deliberate reason.

"What's on the other side of the river?" she asked.

There was a quiet moment before Deedubs said, "Dark territory."

"Sounds ominous," Rose stated, hoping for more, not that she'd get it from him.

Instead, as she suspected, it was Coram who elaborated. "Our land is divided in two halves. On this side of the river is Eppersett. On the other is Widcrook. The two countries have been at war since anyone can remember. It is a dark place filled with monstrous beings who seek nothing but blood and treasure. Yet they are at the mercy of the Abomination same as we are. No one is safe."

"Have you ever been over there?" Rose asked. "Across the bridge and into Widcrook?"

Coram shook his head. "No. Hardly anyone goes over there if it can be avoided. There're only two reasons one would go—war and a death wish. Of us, only Deedubs has ever been there."

Rose looked at the Cobberjack. "Have you really?"

Deedubs grunted as if annoyed, but his head raised slightly, his pride peeking out. But only for a moment. When he spoke, it was in a voice that was gnarled with pain. "Be thankful the weapons we seek aren't on that side, little Rose. We'd stand no chance. I lost my entire army over there. My sight too."

Rose felt her throat constricting. "What . . . what happened?"

Deedubs's lips pulled back, revealing his teeth. "I don't talk about that."

Some of the boats sailing up and down the river looked like living things—huge orange beasts with sails like skin and heads like serpents, populated with crews all along their spines, while others moved with swirling dark clouds above them, which Rose assumed was some kind of magic since engines were not in existence here. There were boats that could have been floating islands—they were filled with thick trees and animals that cried out over the great river. Many vessels were fishing while some were docking in little shanty towns filled with tents and open fires—Coram said these places were up and down the entire river, populated with people fleeing the Abomination, their homes in the south destroyed, their families displaced. On both sides of the river. These unfortunate creatures had run for their lives, hundreds of miles, but there was nowhere to hide for long. Eventually, the Abomination would find them. It would find everyone.

Rose was ashamed of herself. Back home, she had run from far less.

Two hours later, the Order of the Sacrifice stopped along the river to catch their breath and eat some of the food that remained and drink from the river. The water was cool, and it caressed Rose's throat on the way down, her tongue left pleasurably buzzing. But as she came up, wiping her mouth, she caught her reflection in the river, a face materializing over her right shoulder. It was Coram, and he was grinning madly, as if trying to stifle laughter. His arms were extended, his fingers wriggling.

"Oh, no, you don't," Rose yelled. She whipped around and grabbed him by the arms. Then she leaned back, bringing all her weight with her and, placing a foot on his chest, propelled him straight into the river, head over heels.

Quite impressed with herself, she waited for him to come back up so that she could laugh in his face. Oh, was she going to give it to him. She was already giggling like crazy. No way was he getting off that easily.

Only Coram didn't come back up.

"Coram?" The name popped like a bubble. "Coram, don't joke around."

"What did you do?" Ridge cried as he came running over, his breaths heavy. "He can't swim! He's made of gold, Rose! He'll sink!"

Rose's heart plummeted. She leaned over, her panic-scorched eyes searching desperately for him. She plunged her hands deep into the water, the sun casting a brilliant reflection across the rippling surface. It was so strong it almost blinded her eyes, and beneath this intense glow, a shadow dwelled. Rose's eyes widened in hope. "Coram? Coram!" A moment later, his arms came thrusting up out of the shimmer and grabbed hold of Rose's shirt. She saw his face only for a second, a huge grin all the way across it, before she was pulled in after him.

On shore, Ridge and the others dissolved into hysterics. Even Deedubs had a smile on his face. Coram, laughing so hard he was choking on all the water he swallowed, swam to the riverbed and leapt up out of the water as if he had been born in it, his long, thin hair draped across his face, his shirt clinging to his chest.

Flopping around in the river, her body frozen over with shock and anger, Rose cried to Ridge, "You lied to me!"

"A joke!" Ridge said, wiping at his eyes. "A joke! All in good fun!"

Eo, who had not seemed amused at all, hurried over and very carefully lifted Rose out of the water by his teeth. The air snapped at her body, her chin quivered, and her hair was a mess—she moved it from her face, but now it was spiking out from all sides as if she were electrocuted. Coram, his grin somewhat restrained, held out his arms, his fingers waving her in. "Come here. I can warm you up."

"No," Rose said, turning her head away, her chin jutting forward.

"Come on. It'll take two seconds."

"No."

"All this sun has got me burning up, Rose. Don't let it go to waste. Come on."

Still, she refused.

Everyone else was still laughing, and it was as if they needed to so bad. But Rose didn't like the sound of it at all. It reminded her of SallyAnn. It reminded her of home and all the things she was running from. Her instinct was to hide. To dig a hole and climb into it. But instead she spoke up.

"None of this is funny," she said, her arms folded. "People are dying. And it's up to us to do something about it. And if we don't, my brother . . ." Her voice trailed off, unable to finish. "There's nothing funny about it at all." Then she stormed off and sat far away from the group.

Meadowrue followed and took a seat across from her. "Coram's a good fighter," she said. "So good he probably never even thought about dying before this mission. The stakes are very high for him. For all of us. It's very jarring. He doesn't know how to react."

"And I'm supposed to?"

"No. Of course not. But when you find yourself in enough of these situations like I have—all these battles, all these wars, facing down threat after threat after threat—you realize people react in different ways, most of them pretty strange. Dying's natural, but we don't get much practice with it. You can understand that, right?"

Rose nodded. "I guess so. It's just that, I don't know . . . I don't even feel like myself anymore."

"Maybe that's a good thing."

"A good thing?" Rose said.

"They say there's a place hidden somewhere in Eppersett that you could go," Meadowrue said. "A place where you'd find a sorcerer in a cave who could make you someone else. Jundowko. I've always dreamed of finding him. I see myself walking up to him, and I know exactly what I'd say."

"What?" Rose asked, leaning forward.

"I'd say, 'I don't want to be a fairy, but I need to fly. Make me a bird so that I can get lost in the clouds. So I can't hear the noise below. So that I can fly so high everyone becomes a dot on the ground, with no face and no voice and no way to hurt me. Make me a bird so that I can fly past the mountains and find something new.'"

Meadowrue's eyes dropped, and Rose's heart went out to her. She didn't see anything that needed changing. There was nothing wrong with Meadowrue at all.

CHAPTER 15
LEMONWYLL BRIDGE

To Rose Coffin, the bridge was a city, and it was impossible to call it anything else. It had streets and alleys, buildings and homes, places of worship and places to lose one's time. It was full of shops and markets, banks and taverns, squares and parks. It was a lot to traverse, and every passing second was another second of destruction rained down by the Abomination somewhere south of here, getting closer and closer by the day. The faster they found the spiked armor, the faster they could move on to the next weapon, the faster they could end this nightmare.

Setting foot onto the bridge the following morning, Rose couldn't even tell they were standing over water except for the port on either side where all the ships docked, creatures piling out by the hundreds, filling the cobblestone streets that were already overcrowded to the point of suffocation.

In the distance, the city could be seen rising higher and higher as the bridge gradually elevated. Rose figured it would take most of the day to reach the castle at the center.

The population that pushed past her was a wide spectrum of races and personality. There were humanlike people who covered their bodies in brightly colored cloths that bulged and moved. Tiny trolls snorted and elbowed their way through the crowds while other creatures flew over them, Meadowrue gazing up with envy. Books were nailed to the walls, pages flapping, as a voice boomed from along the spine preaching the contents within. There were Centaurs and Minotaurs and cloaked figures that appeared to be concealing nothing but dark smoke and red eyes. There were Willapps and Cobberjacks and creatures of silver and bronze, though no golden boys like Coram.

Banners hung from building to building and lanterns dangled over the sidewalks. There were many beggars rattling their boxes of few coins, and street musicians playing the most unusual of instruments.

The sidewalks were lined with cart after cart loaded with goods for sale, strange aromas lingering in the air around them. The sellers stepped forward into the street showing off what they had, barking their benefits and values. Rose eyed everything closely, slack-jawed at what she saw.

A hunchbacked ogre lifted a meaty kind of substance, shoving it her way, the smell rank. Rose withdrew, her face scrunched up, offending the seller. With a snarl, he wiped his hand across his nose and flung the mucus at her. It missed, but that didn't stop Coram's sword from cutting through the air, settling an inch from the ogre's neck. "Apologize," he said, which the ogre did, his eyes glued to Coram's gold skin. "Now give us some of those thorn slugs before I decide to make my payment in blood."

The ogre filled a bag with the writhing meat and tossed it to him. As Coram handed over the money, the ogre asked, "Ever thought about selling your skin?"

"Haven't you heard? We don't do that anymore," Coram answered, and popped one of the slugs in his mouth and offered the rest to the others. Everyone partook except for Rose, her stomach rumbling for a wide assortment of reasons.

While Rose was unable to look away from the strange sights, most of the eyes on the bridge were looking at Coram. He seemed to shrink under the scrutiny, his eyes darting all over, never lingering in one place for very long. His breaths were as deep as ever, and he was suddenly rather skittish, jumping at every shout and sound, sweat beading across his skin. Eventually, when the group found their path blocked by a large creature, he lunged to pull his sword free once more.

Standing before them was a seven-foot-tall figure with a bird's face—a long, cracked beak, small beady eyes hidden in thick dark feathers that billowed around its long neck. On its back was a large basket filled with objects that moved. The creature held up its hands, a gesture Rose assumed meant it was no threat to them. But it turned out this was how the creature spoke. Protruding from its palms were two small beaks, the two mouths taking turns to speak, one voice far deeper than the other.

"Put the sword away, put the sword away. Just goods here. That's all. That's all."

"What are you selling?" Coram asked, sheathing his sword, though his eyes still carefully scrutinized the merchant.

"Limbs. Extra limbs. Take a look, would you? Go on. Go on." It swung the basket around and Rose peeked in, positive she heard it incorrectly. Inside the wicker, she saw arms and legs, hands and feet, piled upon one another, like a collection from some massacre. The tendons where the limbs and appendages were severed writhed, itching for replacement, the different-colored skins marked and scarred. Repulsed, Rose pulled away.

"We're all fully limbed here, friend!" Ridge said. "Now, move aside! We've business to attend to!"

They tried to push past, but the creature grabbed Coram, its fingers wrapping around his arm, the beak digging in.

"What about you?" the free hand asked.

"What about me?" Coram said, trying to pull free.

"You're going to need to replace that arm. No gold in the basket, but there should be silver."

Coram glanced down. "My arm is fine."

"Is it?"

The crowd was parting behind them, shouts rising up. Rose glanced back, uneasy about the sudden disturbance. What she saw next happened in slow motion.

A man pushed past the onlookers. A human man who could have stepped out of a previous century, his clothes formal and dated. He wore a powdered wig and a leather apron covered with dark stains. His mouth was filled with yellow teeth, and in his hands was the largest sword Rose had ever seen. As he lunged forward through the crowd, he raised it up high.

By the time the sword came down, hacking off Coram's left arm, all Rose could do was scream. This piercing sound—a long and solid note—elicited a wave of energy from her hands that sent the man flying a hundred yards back like a rocket and straight into a building.

In the chaos that followed, someone half Rose's size picked up Coram's arm and ran off with it, darting in and out of the crowd and out of sight. The birdlike creature tried to flee as well, but Ridge grabbed him, frantically dumping out the contents of the basket, as Meadowrue screamed at the merchant that they were the Order of the Sacrifice, which seemed to stun him a bit. Digging through the pile of limbs, Ridge found a silver arm and held it against Coram's exposed wound. "Hold on, mate! The pain'll be gone in a minute!"

Coram had collapsed against the wall, his breathing strained, his eyes opening and closing. "No," he groaned. "No silver. That's not me. That's not me. I'm gold. I'm . . ." His words were lost in a groan.

Rose watched, bewildered, as the loose tendons waved like living tentacles. They were longing to be attached. Soon, the dangling shreds on Coram's shoulder began to react to this new limb, coming to life and seeking a union. The strands reached out, touching one another, rubbing, writhing, until they finally interlocked. Soon, the wound began to close up, gold mixing with silver. Rose couldn't believe what she was witnessing. In a matter of minutes, Coram's arm was completely healed. Looking at his face, however, it was hard to tell he was saved. Stammering, he couldn't remove his eyes from his arm. He attempted to touch the silver but, as if repulsed, pulled away. He mumbled things about who he was, where he came from. He said he was less than whole.

"Not true!" Ridge said. "You have your arm! A good one too! You live to fight another day!"

"Not my arm," Coram said, distant, his eyes distraught. "Silver." He muttered the word over and over again in disbelief. "Silver." It would be a long time before he was on his feet.

With no more to see, the crowds started shifting around them, carrying on with their day. Someone passing by said, "Welcome to Lemonwyll."

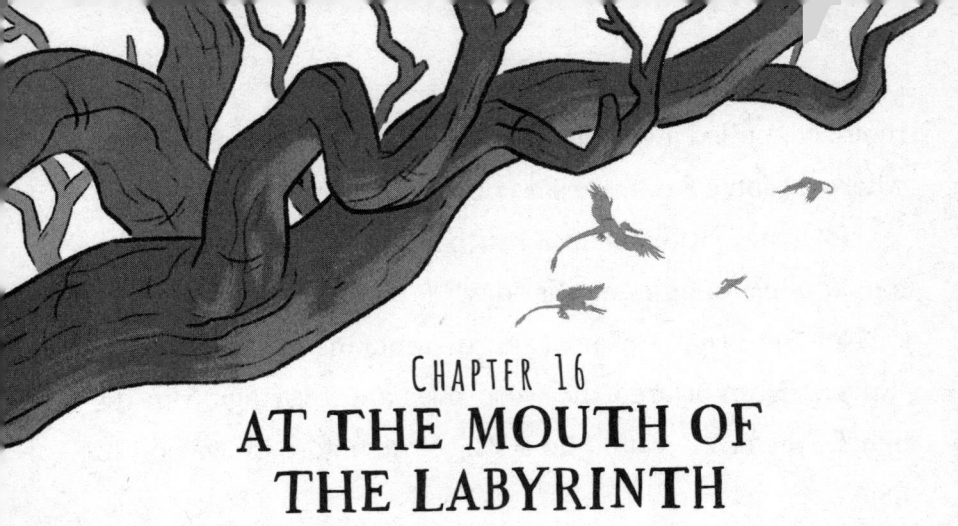

CHAPTER 16
AT THE MOUTH OF
THE LABYRINTH

They reached the castle by nightfall, the labyrinth—and the armor—just below their feet, the bridge just as far behind them as it was ahead. But it was all too clear how weary and battered they all were, the mental strain bearing down hard, and so it was decided that they would try to get some sleep in a nearby inn before setting out in the morning, hopefully refreshed enough to succeed in their quest.

The price was steep at the Squeezed Lemon—the inn-keeper, a man whose bulbous face was hidden in hair, didn't want to house any Cobberjacks, even though Deedubs was suddenly as meek as Eo—but Meadowrue was able to work him down to a reasonable price. Reasonable being

Meadowrue would let him live. As the group paid their money—Ridge couldn't fit through the door with all his branches, and was to sleep outside—the innkeeper leaned over the counter, saying, "Do I know that Cobberjack? Is he—"

"He's my pa," Eo said. "He's old and he's tired, and he would like some sleep. That's all."

The innkeeper scratched at his cheek. "Thought he was that disgrace from way back. The one that failed the entire bridge. You know the one. You must. He was—"

"It's not him," Eo snapped. "That was a different Cobberjack completely."

Deedubs lowered his head and left the room. He didn't speak for the rest of the night, though Eo explained to Rose all about his father's well-known history in Lemonwyll.

"Um, he came here years before I was born. He was leading an army into Widcrook at the time, and for days everyone had been cheering him, and stuft. All along the bridge he ate the greatest foods, slept in the grandest beds. Gifts were laid at his paws. All because he promised them victory against Widcrook. Um, the Widcrook army was threatening to overtake the bridge, and stuft. He told the people here not to flee. He encouraged their young to join him. But his army was poorly trained and out of shape. When they crossed into Widcrook, it was a total slaughter. I think his pride got to him, and stuft. The leader of the dark army was a witch named Bahgdaal. She's the most powerful of all witches, and the only one you will ever meet that has dark red skin. She was the one who blinded him, and after his army was defeated he was forced to walk back across the bridge alone, his head down in shame. It took him days to get across, and every step of the way he heard the calls of the people. He was pelted with food and garbage, he was kicked and clubbed. He walked into every wall and person along the way. He said he changed after that. But I'm not sure how. All I know is that it's taken a lot for him to come back here, and stuft."

An hour later, before a blazing fire in the common room of the inn, Coram was rotating his new arm, as if it were deeply uncomfortable. He flexed his hand and bent it up and down repeatedly, testing the joints, lifting objects up and setting them back down. He twirled his sword, and it flew from his grasp, penetrating the wall by more than half. Although he seemed to be deeply troubled by it all, Rose was in awe at the magic that had taken place.

"Could that be done with anyone?" she asked, swiveling her own arm.

"Mostly," Coram said without picking his head up. He walked to the wall and removed his sword, but he did it with his good arm.

"With any part?"

Coram's eyes shot in her direction. "Wh-what are you getting at?"

Rose looked over at Deedubs, who was already asleep before the fire, curled up like a pup, though his breathing was strained. "If you could get a new arm, why hasn't he received new eyes by now? Or Meadowrue new wings?"

"Oh," Coram said, taking a deep breath.

"Um, when Cobberjacks die, we, um, we rot real quick and stuft. Especially the eyes. It's real difficult to save them."

Rose nodded. "But it could be done."

"Um, I guess. Technically."

"What about you?" Rose asked Meadowrue.

Meadowrue stood up abruptly and headed upstairs to her room. "I don't deserve them."

When Rose heard the door slam, she asked, "Could I receive a new limb? If I needed to?"

Coram plopped down in a chair, his leg up and dangling over the side. "I doubt it. Humans have a much different biology. Besides, it's not much fun. Trust me. Right now my arm is being skinned somewhere in a dark corner of this bridge. And for what? For money. That's why there are so few of us left."

"I'm sorry," Rose said. And she really was. She thought it explained a lot. Because he always lived under the threat of an attack, it was like he could only care about others abstractly. From a distance. He didn't know how to get close to anyone.

"Needless to say, Golddusts don't have the longest life span. It's why I had to learn to fight. It's why I've sought out the best teachers in all of Eppersett. Von Ballard. Goosecheck. The Red Ghost. All my life I've had to defend myself, and I always will. There will never be rest for me. And I will always be alone." He sighed. "The Abomination's destruction will never affect me. My world's already destroyed. But maybe others can have a chance."

The words settled above them like a cloud. Rose wished a wind could come and blow it away. "I know we're not Golddusts," she said, "but we're here with you on this journey. You're not alone."

"This isn't family, Rose. This group, the Order, it isn't even friendship. It's obligation."

Rose lowered her head and stared at her feet. It was strange, his words hurt her. Not very long ago, she was seriously considering using her magic on him. "You're all more friendly to me than anyone back home. Can you believe that? I mean, what's that say about me? The closest thing I've got to friends are the ones who are bringing me to my death."

Coram looked away, eyes on the wood-beamed ceiling. "Rose, it can't be that bad, where you came from."

"Recently I thought I was going to have a friend. For a hot minute, anyway. Her name is SallyAnn, and she's one of the coolest girls in school. I mean, the way she dresses, the way she talks, the confidence . . . I swear she could have her own reality show on TV."

"A reality show? What's TV?"

Rose grinned; for a minute there, she had forgotten where she was. "TV, computers, they're these screens where we get most of our information."

"Like books."

"Not exactly. Anyway, it turned out SallyAnn didn't want to be my friend. She just wanted to humiliate me. Still does. That's why I ran."

"Why would she want to humiliate you?"

"I don't know. I think somehow it makes her more popular."

"I don't like this SallyAnn."

"You and me both. I mean, I guess that's one good thing about never going back. I never have to see her stupid face again."

"I'm sure she has the stupidest face of all."

"It is. It's, like, so stupid."

They both laughed for a moment, and then Coram said, "Rose, I really am sorry."

"For what?"

He leaned forward, hands clasped together, looking directly

at her. "I'm sorry that you ever came here. I'm sorry that home was so tough for you that you had to run. I'm sorry there was no one to help you. You deserve more."

Rose felt as if her mind somersaulted inside her head. Nothing felt right; everything was mixed up, upside down, inside out. She nodded, biting her lip. "Thank you."

There was a long silence between them, until Coram stood up. "It's late," he said. "You should get to bed. Tomorrow is going to be like nothing we have ever experienced, and you need to be ready. If we fail to find the armor, we fail everyone. The Abomination wins. Your magic won't work without the three weapons."

Deedubs was left undisturbed in front of the fire while Eo slept at the foot of Rose's bed in as tight a ball as possible, his back folded perfectly into the concave nook her legs made. The Cobberjack could probably feel her shaking through the night, and maybe that was why he threw a paw over her. Rose never missed her bed more than when she was sleeping somewhere else.

By morning, the group should have all been refreshed, but it was painfully clear, to Rose at least, that they weren't. Their eyes were bloodshot, their bodies were wobbly, their hair stood on end. *And if they look like that, imagine what you look like.* She quickly tried to adjust her appearance with a hand through her hair.

The group all knew what was coming and the dread of it all had obliterated their sleep and ransacked their sense of calm. Hardly a word passed their lips as they made their way from the inn to the castle, the beating of their hearts and the rattling of their bones doing all the talking for them.

Lemonwyll Castle was nothing like Summercress Castle. Unlike Queen Sequoia's impenetrable fortress, this one was swarming with life, its gates open to everyone. Even in the early morning, the castle was still humming with the energy from the night before.

To get to the labyrinth, they had to bypass the boisterous crowds and descend deep into the castle through the dungeon. The prisoners there appeared forgotten, wasted away, half of them hanging by their arms or chained to the wall, shivering with cold. Coram explained how evil and monstrous these prisoners were, but Rose still felt pity for them and she even said so.

Beyond a wood door in a long-abandoned part of the dungeon was a final staircase. It was already dark and cool in these depths, but now, the lower they went, it was becoming unbearable. As they descended the stairs, iridescent rodents crawled across their feet, and Rose exploded in shivers. The critters were hairy and swollen, and they glowed in all sorts of different colors like skittering orbs illuminating the entire staircase. Panatoos, Meadowrue called them.

After the chill ran its course, Rose followed everyone else down the stairs, careful with her steps. At the bottom, she saw a wall in the distance lit by torches, eight doors built into it, leading to the labyrinth beyond.

The ancient maze was carved into the thick concrete of the bridge. No one knew how big it was, who built it, or for what purpose. But at some point in time, an eccentric warlock named Syedel entered through one of the doors and conquered the fire demon that had been imprisoned deep within the labyrinth's center. Legend had it that after this incredible victory, he used the labyrinth to hide all sorts of priceless treasures he had collected in his travels, filling the halls with dangerous creatures to guard them. When his death eventually neared, he returned and died somewhere within. For centuries it had borne his name, and there had been quests in search of his body and the spiked armor, but no one had ever been able to find it. Or, if they did, they never made it out alive.

Standing guard outside the doors were two Minotaurs. They stood like walls, tall and thick, silent and immovable. In their hands were axes twice the size of Rose. Though they clearly saw the group's approach, the monsters didn't speak. The only sound was the air blowing from their nostrils like huge gusts of wind.

"Which door?" Meadowrue whispered to the group.

The doors looked heavy and made of copper that had now oxidized. Each one was the same as the other down to the intricate border, except for the Gothic knockers, which were all unique. Rose had the suspicion the doors hadn't been opened many times, certainly not recently.

After some deliberation, the group decided on the second door from the left—the one with a withdrawn, humanlike face for a knocker—but when they went to open it, one of the Minotaurs blocked their path, its ax swiping down in a flash just ahead of them. The blade was buried deep into the ground. Had it connected, it most likely would have cleaved one of them in half.

"One per door," the Minotaur said.

The group looked at one another, a bit perplexed. "We can't go in together?" Ridge asked.

"Not through the same door," the Minotaur stated, its voice so deep it could have come from beneath its cloven hooves. "This is Syedel's labyrinth. We follow his rules. You conquer it, you can make whatever rules you'd like. We'd even name it after you."

"But we're the Order of the Sacrifice!" Ridge shouted. "We need that armor to stop the Abomination once and for all!"

The Minotaurs, however, remained silent.

The group stepped back and huddled. "This is all they know," Coram said. "All they've ever known. We have to do as they say and split up." He looked into the eyes of the entire group. "Is that okay with all of you?"

Meadowrue nodded. "It'll increase our odds."

"Of what? Dying?" Rose asked.

"You don't have to go in if you don't want," Coram said. "Any of you."

"No one is staying behind," Deedubs said. "The armor is of too great importance."

There was agreement all around, save for one.

"Rose?" Coram asked, his eyes burrowing straight into her.

She felt her pulse quicken. Reality bore down hard. She couldn't do this. Not alone. *You have your voice, Rose. That's all you need. Do it. For your brother.* She swallowed hard. "I'll . . . I'll go."

Coram nodded, a look of admiration on his face. "Okay, then. That settles it. We find the armor and get the heck out; meet here on the other side."

One by one, they picked a door and stood before it. Coram took the door the group had originally selected, Ridge to his left, Meadowrue to his right. Rose, meanwhile, was on the far end, with Deedubs and Eo beside her.

"The Cobberjacks must separate," one of the Minotaurs

said, its tail whipping around as if swatting flies, its head lowered so that the horns pointed accusingly at them.

"But he's blind!" Rose shouted.

"And Syedel had no legs. What of it?" the Minotaur snorted.

Deedubs pulled himself free of the leash and said, "I have my scent. It will carry me through."

Eo was trembling, the leash thrown on his back. "But, Pa—"

"No, Eo. Never in my life have I turned down a challenge, and I won't start now." And he slowly but surely made his way to an unoccupied door. Watching him go, Rose wasn't sure who she was worried for more, father or son.

"Okay, then," Coram said. "Ready?"

They placed their hands on the knockers, Eo and Deedubs rising to two feet, their teeth taking hold instead.

At the count of three, they all knocked twice upon their doors—twelve deep cracks. The ceiling crumbled above them and the hinges squeaked with an asylum's terror as the doors opened wide. Inside was nothing but darkness.

"But we can't see," Rose said, glancing up at the Minotaur.

"Looks like you're all blind now." And then it shoved her in and closed the door, its bellowing laughter cut abruptly short.

Chapter 17
SYEDEL'S LABYRINTH, PART ONE

Rose stood in utter darkness. It was so complete, it was as if it had a presence, a predatory force that backed her up against the door she had entered through, pinning her there. Her heart pounded against her chest, the hands of darkness around her. She could feel its breath, its dominance. It was so easy to give in.

What were you thinking coming in here, Rose? You think you're some kind of fighter now? Some kind of hero? You're a sacrifice. Get it straight.

Rose felt the darkness penetrate her. It crept down her mouth and seeped through her pores. It was filling the space around her bones, from her feet all the way to her skull. It wanted to silence her. Erase her.

And that she couldn't allow. "I have my voice," she said.

Oh, and what good is that going to do right now? You can't see a thing.

Rose pushed herself off the wall, refusing to succumb. If she was going to die, then she'd die fighting. She stepped into the darkness, and it was as if something gave. Each step forward became easier and easier, the enemy in rapid retreat. Her hand traced the wall, fingertips brushing the stone, and it was like claws against her attacker's skin. When she came upon a gap, she stopped and felt for the turn. It was an effective method for now. But she couldn't do this the entire time. What if she came across the armor? She wouldn't even know it. And what if something was sneaking up behind her? What if something was there right now?

She turned around, her entire body shaking as she waited to be struck down. Hands waving, she reached out into the darkness, her body circling.

Nothing.

Long exhale.

Okay, keep moving.

But suddenly, she had lost her sense of direction. *Shoot. You got all turned around. Which way were you headed,*

Rose? There were plenty of noises all around her. They echoed throughout the labyrinth like the dark's chattering teeth. Rose had no idea what was making them or how close they actually were. At times, it even sounded like some of the walls were moving.

But as she stood there glaring down the darkness, she thought she saw something. The faintest of lights. She rubbed her eyes, hoping to adjust them back to her dark reality. But it turned out there really was a glow in the center of the darkness. A tiny ball of light. It was bright orange and jumped around in the pitch, gaining in intensity.

"A Panatoo," Rose whispered, a tinge of awe in her voice.

She walked toward the iridescent rodent, a hand bracing the wall. Quietly, she called out to it as if it were a cat. She said she had food, a warm bed. But nothing worked. Every time she got close, the Panatoo scurried farther into the distance.

She wanted to get her hands on it—she needed to—but there was no way she was going to be able to catch it. Not like this.

Then she was struck with an idea. Maybe she could make it come to her.

Kneeling down in the dark, Rose began to sing. It wasn't like she did when she was attacking the flying snake or the satellite in the Field of Stylites. These weren't weaponized screams or long, fiery notes of violence. This was like singing with her brother. There was beauty and hope in her voice. It was a song.

In the dark of the labyrinth, she sang for the Panatoo to come near. She sang for it to not be afraid, that she was a friend. She sang from deep within herself. And sure enough, the Panatoo stopped running, caught in the song's trance. Gradually, it turned around and began to skitter closer and closer, nose raised in the air, taking in her scent. Rose held out her hands, and after a brief moment of hesitation and some more sniffing, the Panatoo crawled right into them, a ball of light in her palms.

Rising to her feet, she pet the rodent repeatedly, the hairs long and bristly, each one aglow, the tips nearly white. It turned out it wasn't much like a rat after all. It was actually kind of cute. Large, round eyes that popped far out of its head, a nose that curled back on itself and wiggled, and a mouth full of tiny crooked teeth, an inner light shining out between them. It was warm and fuzzy, and that was exactly how it made Rose feel.

"Okay," she said. "Maybe now we can actually get somewhere in this place."

With the light in her hands, she could see several feet in all directions now, and sure enough, the walls really were moving. Some of them. There were also staircases all about, some leading up, some down. There were even trapdoors in the ceilings and floors.

"Great," she said. "As if this wasn't challenging enough."

After a brief moment of hesitation, she decided to stick to the path she was currently on, walking a little longer until she eventually hit a dead end. "Hmm." She spun around. "I thought this was open a minute ago." She raised the Panatoo to her face. "Didn't you think it was open? Yeah, I know you did." She heard a sound nearby and realized a wall was moving. "Fine. We'll just go this way, then." But after a few steps toward the opening, the Panatoo started writhing in her hands. It squeaked and tried to run, almost jumping off the tips of her fingers. Rose gathered it in close, petting its bristles, saying that everything was okay. But as the stones slowly slid away, she realized why the Panatoo was skittish: Something was standing in the opening.

The creature was so tall its head was tilted against the ceiling. Whatever it was, it was skeletal, but with its organs showing, its veins and muscles, as if the skin had not yet developed.

The wall was slow to open, but having seen them, the creature was now anxious. It placed its hands against the opening and pushed, a moan coming from its distorted mouth.

The Panatoo shrieked, its face burrowing in fear against Rose's chest.

"You don't have to tell me twice!" Rose shouted to her new friend, and bolted down the hall.

The monster was now free and staggering closer. It let out a ravenous groan, its feet making a suction sound that chased her down. Its veins extended, stretching out from its body. They pulled at the walls to gain more speed, the creature's breathing loud and hoarse.

Even with the Panatoo, it was still difficult to see ahead. She held it forward, trying to get as much light as possible, but when running like this, she was bound to hit a wall or fall down some stairs. Especially as she kept glancing back.

The monster was gaining, its veins flailing in the air like writhing fingers reaching out for Rose.

Find a wall that's closing, she thought. *Jump in at the last second. It'll never be able to follow you.*

It was a pretty good plan, if she had to say so herself and, in fact, a moment later, she heard one shifting shut. It wasn't far ahead. Judging by the sound, it was just another ten yards or so. She made for it, tucking the Panatoo like a football. A moment later, the opening became clear. There wasn't much room left, but she thought she could make it. It would be a tight squeeze, but she was small enough. Charging, she ducked her head and was about to jump into the narrow opening, when she ran right smack into a second beast. She collapsed to the ground, and all she knew was that she wouldn't be making it to the Abomination. Her death was far more imminent than that.

CHAPTER 18

SYEDEL'S LABYRINTH, PART TWO

*S*tay down."

Deedubs said it to Rose as he leapt clear over her. Soaring through the dank air of the labyrinth, he unleashed a hellish howl. All four paws were stretched out, claws popped, teeth bared. When he landed, it was hard against the monster's chest. Together, they slammed to the ground.

"Deedubs!" Rose cried.

The Cobberjack was thrown against the wall, and the monster stood. Once again, the veins from its arms extended, quickly wrapping themselves around Deedubs's legs, binding him. The Cobberjack tried ripping them with his teeth, but for every strand he snapped, a dozen more kept coming. Soon, his snout was bound. Then his torso. Then every remaining inch of his body.

Rose let go of the Panatoo, and it retreated up her arm and down the back of her shirt. Slowly, she backed away, but the wall behind her was now sealed. Deedubs was completely engulfed, his body slowly being dragged on the ground toward the monster for consumption.

Sing, Rose thought. *Sing for your life! Sing for his!* With her back against the wall and her hands extended outward, she opened her mouth and let out a note. A short, sharp blast came from her hands, and it must have been painful because the creature shrieked. Then, in defense, it quickly wrapped its veins around Rose's throat. Her voice was cut off, and soon all her oxygen would be too. The pressure was incredible. Her hands shot up and tried to rip the veins away, but it was no use. Her eyesight was fading. Her body was weakening.

The creature stumbled closer, its skeletal jaw opening wide, a pulsing tongue exposed. Terrified, Rose dropped her eyes to its chest, and there she saw the beating of its heart. It pumped there beneath its rib cage. Her hand reached out for it, but her wrist was quickly bound by more veins. Her fingertips brushed against the organ but couldn't grab it, and her arm was flung back against the wall and tied there. The creature was now only inches from her face. Its veins wrapped around her entire body, head to toe, just like Deedubs. Her face was engulfed, her body squeezed tight. The creature pulled her in. Their chests touched. Rose was close to blacking out, she could feel it. She screamed, but her cry barely left her lungs. And that's when she felt the Panatoo skitter down her arm. Through her last crack of consciousness, through a small space between the veins that bound her, she watched as the critter ravenously burrowed straight for the creature's heart. Its glow was bright and the more it ate, the brighter it glowed. The creature stiffened with surprise. Its hand lunged for the Panatoo but couldn't reach. Its veins went in search, but it was too late. The Panatoo had reached the heart and began to eat a hole clean through it. The creature's legs wobbled. One knee hit the ground, then the other. A second later, the creature fell on its face, the veins loosening around Rose.

Writhing, gasping for breath, she threw them off and Deedubs did the same. Then she crawled over and, with a trembling hand, reached out and petted the Cobberjack, stroking his fur.

"Thank you," she said, unable to look at the horror at their feet.

Deedubs shook his body dry, spraying Rose with a fine red mist, and stepped away from the corpse. "Don't thank me," he said, breathing heavily. "Don't thank anyone. We still have a long way to go and however difficult it is to find the armor, defeating whatever guards it will be even more so. Truthfully, I expected you to be dead already. That or cowering behind the door you entered."

"You're so sweet," Rose said.

"Tell me, how did you manage to get this far in the dark?"

Rose told him about the glowing Panatoo she lured and carried around. In response, Deedubs said he only hoped the rest of the group were so ingenious, giving her a thrilling jolt that ran straight through her body and lingered somewhere in her toes. Rose told him she decided to name the Panatoo Orange Blossom, and Deedubs declared it a horrible moniker. "Pray it doesn't understand you," he said. "Or you might lose your fingertips in its mouth. You need to give that thing a proper name. A warrior's name! It saved your life!"

"Yours too," Rose added, a sharp blow to Deedubs's pride.

But Rose insisted on the name's relevance as the animal was orange and looked like a flower in full bloom. "It's as good a name as any," she said. "Especially in this place."

"Do you mean the labyrinth or Eppersett?"

"Does it matter?"

"I suppose you think the name Rose is so great too," he said with a sniff.

"It's not horrible."

"A rose is easily trampled and ripped to shreds, with only the tiniest of thorns to protect itself. And it will never get anywhere unless it is cut down first."

"Uh, that's one metaphor, I guess. It also stands for love."

Deedubs snorted and padded through the darkness. Looking down at her new pet, Rose thought, *No name is going to decide what we can be. Right?* She held the animal up to her eyes, cocked her head, and smiled at it. To her, it seemed like it smiled back.

As time went on, Orange Blossom grew more and more comfortable with Rose, stretching out in her hands, even dozing off from time to time, though that meant its glow faded and Rose had to continuously shake it awake. "Sorry, Blossom," she kept telling the Panatoo. Either it really couldn't understand her, or it didn't mind Orange Blossom for a name, because it never snapped, not even when it was so clearly tired. Maybe it actually liked her, she thought.

For hours they went up stairs and down stairs, through sliding walls and back in circles, all while fighting off countless creatures that appeared out of the darkness. At least Deedubs did. Rose just watched him, partially in awe, partially in terror. There were trolls and zombies, giant spiders and things that walked across the ceiling with eight tentacles.

For all of them, Deedubs was so quick, so vicious and precise. Not once did Rose feel she needed to aide him. Even without his sight, he was incredibly deadly, and she wondered what kind of a warrior he must have been back when he was young.

"Did your father teach you to fight?" she asked shortly after Deedubs disabled a bat-like creature that had dropped down from the ceiling.

"Every Cobberjack is taught by their father."

Rose thought how her father taught her that fighting was only a last resort. Would she be different if he had been more like Deedubs? Would SallyAnn have then steered clear of her? Or would it not have mattered? Maybe Rose was always going to be who she was. After all, Eo didn't seem to be taking after *his* father. "So, you've taught Eo how to fight?" she asked.

Deedubs snorted. "As much as that pup can be taught."

"Are you worried about him in here alone?"

"I prepared him the best I can. Unfortunately he doesn't have the heart of a fighter."

Rose winced. "I think Eo *is* a fighter. Just a different kind than you."

"There's only one kind, Rose, and he's not it. Trust me. I don't need eyes to see it. You're more of a warrior than he'll ever be. If you ever wake up to it."

Again, Rose felt a swell of pride, though she hardly believed it. "I don't know. Hurting someone? I don't like it."

"You don't have to like it to be good at it."

"Well, there must be a better way to bring peace."

Deedubs somehow met her eyes. "Tell that to the Abomination before it devours you."

CHAPTER 19
SYEDEL'S LABYRINTH,
PART THREE

As they continued on through the labyrinth, Rose felt the oppression of the walls. They closed in on her even as the maze seemed to expand. It was no different than the darkest recesses of her mind. *Places like this shouldn't exist*, she thought.

"How do you do this?" she asked Deedubs. "An entire life filled with fighting and killing. It's no way to live."

"I know what you think of me," he said. "What most do. You believe I'm a heartless killer. And, yes, maybe I do relish in the blood of victory, but I'm no monster, Rose. To be a truly great fighter, one must have a purpose, and it can't be a selfish one. I do what I do to save others. This mission we're on? It is a worthy one. I will gladly die for it. And that's where Eo differs from me. He fears death. His own. Fear is all about the self. Once you let that go, once you care more for others than you do for yourself, that's when you become a true hero."

Rose didn't respond. His words were still taking hold within her. She felt them shifting around, searching for a place to settle, to embed themselves. Something told her they'd be around for a while.

By now she had lost all track of time. They could have been in the labyrinth for hours or even days for all she knew. She felt tired and weak, aged by the darkness. Even Deedubs was slowing down. Each fight had taken its toll on him, and there had been many. He had numerous wounds across his body. She wasn't sure how much longer they would last. Not that he complained. Not once. And that made Rose keep quiet too, no matter how much her bones ached.

They turned down yet another path—was this the hundredth? thousandth?—their feet dragging along with their spirits. There had been points in the journey that she heard cries somewhere within the labyrinth. They were impossible to track, but her heart filled with dread at the sounds of one of her friends in trouble.

This gave her pause. It was the second time she had thought of them as friends. Were they? Since they'd first met, they had had no desire but to sacrifice her to the Abomination.

They were risking their lives too, but that didn't automatically make them friends, did it? What if Rose wasn't willing to sacrifice herself to save her brother? How kind would they be then? Probably not at all. So why did she care so much whether they survived this labyrinth or not? Was it because she needed them to cure her brother? Or was it deeper than that? She glanced over at Deedubs. Even he had grown on her.

She shook her head, unsure what it all meant. It wasn't like she had a long history of friends to draw from. *Maybe this is the best you get, Rose. The only people who will talk to you are the ones escorting you to the end.*

Another turn, another flight of stairs, up then down, another turn, a dead end, a secret door, another turn. One after another after another after another.

"I've had enough of this!" she shouted, kicking the wall. "We're never getting out of here! What ever made us think we could defeat the Abomination? We can't even get through the first challenge!" Her tantrum took an abrupt turn, and she grew more somber. "I don't want to be here anymore. I wish I were home. I wish I were sitting on my couch in sweats with a cup of hot chocolate and some cookies, school canceled due to snow, the TV on to one of my favorite shows, the Christmas tree up in the corner of the room, that flickering glow of the lights."

"You're speaking gibberish. Do you need to rest?"

"I need to get out of here. I need my brother to wake up. I need my parents back, if only for a little bit. I need a million things. I need—"

The words froze in Rose's mouth as, up ahead, she spotted something at the far end of the path. "What the . . . ?"

"What is it?" Deedubs asked, his nose in the air.

"Something's . . . glowing. It's far off. Could be two hundred feet away, maybe more. Looks gold."

"Probably another Panatoo."

"But it's not moving."

Deedubs stopped, raising his nose higher. Rose waited, watching him. He took a few steps forward and sniffed for some time, a look of confusion crossing his face.

"Well?" she asked.

"You're right. It's not a Panatoo. It's not anything else we've come across either."

"Then what is it?"

"I'm not sure. In all my travels, I've never come along a scent like this." Tentatively, he walked forward. "Be on your guard."

They crept closer and closer, but still there was no movement to the golden glow. With each step they took, it only grew brighter. Rose felt drawn to it immediately, unable to move her eyes away for even a second. Her pace quickened; she began to sweat.

Soon, she could make the object out clearly. It appeared to be a metal cape covered in six-inch spikes. It was draped over a skeleton, a skeleton without any legs.

"The armor," she said.

Deedubs froze. "Rose, are you sure?"

"Has to be."

"Then don't move."

"But we have to grab it."

"It won't be that simple."

"There's nothing around, Deedubs. I'm looking everywhere. We're okay."

Deedubs's nose was wet with use. "Don't. Move."

From beyond the armor, something was snaking their way. It moved along the floor in a zigzag pattern, sliding toward them like a fat worm.

"Back," Deedubs said.

But Rose was just staring. It looked harmless enough. A little gelatinous blob. It was almost hypnotic how it moved, its girth shifting from back to front. She couldn't take her eyes off it.

"Back."

The slug passed the armor, draping over the skeleton, and moved toward them still. It seemed like it was growing now. Larger and thicker.

"Back!"

The worm picked up speed. In no time at all, it was charging them. Rose turned to run, but out of the corner of her eye, she watched in terror as the blob slowly rose up from the floor.

What she thought was a worm was actually the top of a creature's head. An ugly, bubbling thing. It had a human form but barely, its entire crooked body pulsing and bubbling. Its face was like a sick elephant's, its trunk fat and drooping low—there was a strange gurgling sound coming from it, one that turned Rose's stomach. The monster was hunched over, leaning heavily on a staff made of the very same material as its body.

"What is that thing?" Rose said.

"Quick. Describe it to me."

Rose did the best she could in the quickest time possible, and Deedubs nodded in reverence. "I have heard of the Kilsun legend since I was a pup. I had always dreamed of one day facing it. Now it seems that time has come. A good day."

Kilsun was gazing at the floor. Its trunk swayed. Subtly, at first, then more violently. Back and forth, back and forth. Its entire body joining in. With a sudden jerk, its head and chest lunged forward, like something was caught in its throat. There was a terrible gagging sound, and soon the trunk was throbbing. Three large objects slowly made their way down, one after another. When they reached the tip, the trunk spread wide, and out squeezed three gelatinous balls. They fell and rolled across the ground, rapidly growing in size. One foot in circumference, then two feet, three feet, four . . . until they suddenly burst open.

Out of the blobs came what looked like razor-backed wolves. Their eyes red and large, their mouths overstuffed with teeth as jagged and sharp as their fur. They were salivating just looking at Rose and Deedubs. And when Kilsun issued some garbled call behind them—like an underwater shout—they charged.

"For the armor!" Deedubs cried in response. "For Eppersett!" And with a roar, he charged too.

In a wild clash, he took on all three wolves at once, smacking them aside and tearing at their stomachs. It was as if he instinctively knew where they were vulnerable, the scent of blood so forceful in his nose.

Kilsun, meanwhile, backed away. Hunched against its staff, it appeared to be gagging again.

It's trying to drum up more of those . . . those . . . things, Rose thought, her mind frantic. *Do something!*

Panicking, she let out a thudding note. With the familiar tingle coursing through her body and fingers, a blast appeared from her hands and shot across the dark hall like a comet. Kilsun, however, merely waved its staff and the blast deflected, killing one of its own wolves instead.

Rose was startled. *What, you thought you were all power-ful or something? Get him again!* This time she tried a higher note, a more powerful delivery, but this too was deflected.

Her body weakened. She had expended too much too quickly. She was already tired and now these conjurings were draining her fast. Meanwhile, Kilsun was gagging again. Its trunk filled. And then it spat. The blobs rolled along the floor, gaining in size as they neared. Soon, more wolves joined the fray.

Deedubs was losing ground. Four wolves lay dead at his feet, but it was clear he wouldn't survive if more kept coming. His body was all torn up, his paws ripped open. Rose had to do something, and she had to do it now.

It was going to drain her completely, but she had to try. With her body arched forward, she screamed with an anger she had been reserving for SallyAnn. A massive blast emerged from her hands, a blast so big it knocked her back as it shot Kilsun's way. The creature tried to deflect it, but the force shattered the staff into countless pieces. Rose, meanwhile, collapsed.

With a chance to finish her, Kilsun rushed toward Rose, its entire body lunging and swaying. Deedubs, sensing the threat, jumped to her defense. But with surprisingly quick movements, Kilsun caught him in midair by the throat. It squeezed hard, forcing Deedubs's mouth wide open. Like a worm, its trunk found its way to the open maw and released a ball down his throat.

Deedubs dropped to the ground, writhing and pawing at his stomach. The wolves were dead, but his fight was far from over.

With nothing else in its way, Kilsun stood over Rose. Inches from her face, the trunk snorted, a warm mist enveloping her skin.

Kilsun bent down and, after swatting Orange Blossom aside, grabbed Rose's throat. Rose tried to keep her mouth closed, but it was no use. She choked for air. In the dank darkness of the labyrinth, Kilsun's trunk snaked forward and found her lips. Pushing past, it soon began to pulse.

Rose's eyes bulged as she saw the trunk widen, the ball making its way down. She tried swatting at it, but her arms could barely move. She kicked, but her legs found nothing but air. She tried to bite, but her jaw was open much too wide.

You're dead, Rose. It ends here. It all ends here.

It was then that Rose saw Deedubs leap against Kilsun, knocking it to the ground, a tremendous roar filling the labyrinth. He fought with a fury she had never seen, a crazed viciousness. She couldn't believe he still had such strength in him. How? It was impossible. How did he manage it?

Her eyes drifted over to where Deedubs had been writhing in pain, and she had to blink twice because what she saw confused her. Deedubs was still there, the fight slowly leaving his body. Looking back at Kilsun, everything became clear. It wasn't Deedubs who was tearing it to pieces. It was Eo.

In that moment, he had become his father, a ruthless fighter, determined and sure. Kilsun, it turned out, didn't have a chance. Its trunk was up in the air, a muted sound bellowing from within. With a guttural roar, Eo raised his paw and sliced the thing in two. It flopped there on the ground, slowly deflating until it was nothing but a small blob. Helpless, Kilsun raised its arms, one last desperate attempt at survival. But Eo showed it no mercy. Three more swipes of his claws, and Kilsun never moved again.

With the body shrinking at his paws, Eo gave a quick glance over to Rose to make sure she was okay, then hurried to his father, his paws caressing his father's head.

"Pa . . ."

"You defeated him, Eo," Deedubs said, his pride in his son shining through. "The armor is yours."

"Pa . . ."

"You are a warrior. You have become what you were always meant to be, my son. You fight for something bigger than yourself now. You . . . you will guide Rose all the way to the end. You will save Eppersett."

"Pa . . ."

Rose crawled over, her face pale at the sight of Deedubs rocking from side to side, his teeth clenched in anguish. "It's a . . . a good death," he said. "I accept it."

"No, you can't," Eo cried.

"I do. And so . . . so should you. Just . . . just do me one thing, Eo."

"Anything, Pa."

"Carry me back across the bridge. Let them know . . . Let them know I tried to make things right."

"Pa, I need you, and stuft. I need you."

"No, you don't. Not anymore. I . . . I love you, my boy."

Deedubs's eyes opened impossibly wide, his mouth agape though no sound came. Eo dropped at his dead father's side and wept. Rose, her heart unbearably heavy, put her arms around the two Cobberjacks, father and son, the living and the dead, and wept too.

Chapter 20
FUNERAL MARCH

It was Eo's armor to take, and it fit him perfectly, locking around his neck and draping across his long back like a cape. It was as if it were made for him. The moment he grabbed it and put it on, a door opened in the floor, just behind Syedel's skeleton, stairs that disappeared into the darkness below. Eo asked Rose to hold the armor so that he could carry his father's body across his back and out of the labyrinth. Rose obliged, and together, they climbed down the stairs and made their way along a hallway that never offered any alternate paths, no sliding walls, no hidden creatures. It should have felt like a victory lap, but Deedubs's death made it a funeral march.

Eventually, the hall led them all the way to the eight entrances of the labyrinth. There, they found the others waiting for them, and Rose was elated to see nobody else had suffered as Deedubs had, though they did look a little worse for wear—Coram's new arm hung limp, Meadowrue was covered in bruises to the point she was almost completely purple, and Ridge had lost more than half his branches, thick wedges cleaved deep into his trunk as if something had attempted to chop him down, and more than two-thirds of his birds were gone. Apparently when the armor was found, doors were opened leading them out as well.

The looks on their faces seeing Deedubs's body were something Rose would never forget. It was such a raw and powerful thing to witness. Ridge was openly weeping, and Coram couldn't stop rubbing his hand along the fallen Cobberjack's neck, stating how he didn't get to say goodbye, how he never told Deedubs how much he respected him. Meadowrue couldn't even bear to look his way; she turned around almost immediately, her head down, her fists clenched. As Rose looked on, she felt strangely connected to them. Death had the ability to both push and pull.

Orange Blossom sat on her shoulder, nuzzling against her neck. Three times she tried returning the animal to its home in the labyrinth, but the creature wouldn't leave, and this cheered Rose up some. She had always wanted a pet, and right now she could definitely use one.

When the group was ready to depart, the Minotaurs blocked their path, their axes coming down before Rose. "You have the armor," one said. "The labyrinth belongs to you now."

Rose shook her head and nodded toward Eo. "No. It's his. He defeated Kilsun."

The Minotaurs turned, their bodies straightening. They dropped to their knees before Eo. "We are yours to command. By right, you can do what you wish with the labyrinth. Tell us, and it will be done. Anything."

Eo gave a quick glance to Rose, who nodded at him.

Without glancing back at the doors, he said, "Um, tear it down and stuft. Tear it all down."

The Minotaurs looked puzzled, even a little saddened. "But . . . but what about us?"

"You're free," Eo said.

The Minotaurs nodded, saying his will would be carried out. Before Rose even made it up the stairs to the castle, she could already hear them chopping away at the walls with their axes.

As Eo carried his father through the crowds, the reaction on Lemonwyll Bridge was immediate. Everyone paid close attention, coming to a standstill in the middle of every street as they passed. Once the shock and whispers subsided, once the truth had spread, heads were bowed. Some onlookers even took to their knees. Through it all, Rose noticed Eo's eyes welling up. She noticed how, even under the strain, his stride straightened, his chin raising to the sky. He radiated pride.

Eo found a space along the river's edge, just beneath where the bridge began to rise, and started to dig. He refused any help, his paws tearing at the ground at a feverish pace. When he was done with the hole, he placed his father in, the body practically falling apart at the touch. After sealing the grave, as everyone gathered around, he said a few words.

"Um, I know how my pa was, and stuft. How he could be real hard and mean. He wasn't always the nicest, even to me. But he lived a hard life, with a lot of hard lessons thrown at him. And he wanted to pass those lessons on to me in a hard way, but nothing like what he experienced. I could always feel him holding back, and stuft. I know I never lived up to my pa's expectations, and stuft. But that doesn't mean I'm out of time. I'm going to see this through to the end. I promise him that much."

Later, with a small fire going and everyone getting some much needed rest, Coram reminded them of what lay ahead.

"The arrows of Millenten are buried in the Cemetery of Bad Dreams." He said this with a catch in his throat, his eyes avoiding Meadowrue. "To get there, we're going to have to abandon the river for a bit. The Cemetery is inland from here. It shouldn't take us very long to reach it. A day or two at most."

Rose was aching for sleep, but her mind was still reeling from the day's events and what was to come. She glanced over at Meadowrue, who had been silent the entire night. She held her head, as if another ball might come rolling out, her face pale beneath the bruises.

Rose thought about how she would have liked a chance to bury her own bad dreams. Bury them deep. But then she realized what it must be like for Meadowrue, when you've buried so many and were now going to dig them all back up. Nightmares never stayed buried for long. Soon enough, they had to be faced.

CHAPTER 21
AN OFFER ON THE TABLE

Shortly after sunrise the following morning, the Order came across a strange figure sitting in a chair in a grass field in the middle of nowhere. There was also a second chair, as well as a small fold-out table, deeply worn. Sitting on the table was a glass canister, and trapped inside the canister was a withering fairy.

The group approached cautiously, weapons drawn, unsure what was awaiting them.

The figure had no defining shape, just a long, slender body, with stubble for hair and arms and legs that extended a tad too far. It wore high black boots that were covered in dirt, holes in the soles, buckles that didn't buckle. The rest of its clothes were also raggedy, falling apart at the seams. The figure sat awkwardly, twisted upon itself and bent over, though its head was raised, its piercing blue eyes staring right at them. It all looked rather painful, like something was trapped inside its body, contorting it. The skin that showed through the holes was bright white, like milk or paint. There were splotches of the figure's natural color peeking through, but the white had overtaken much of the body, traveling all the way up the neck and engulfing most of its face. It was the Abomination's disease. And this victim was near death.

When they were close enough, the figure gestured across the table to the empty seat.

"We don't wish to sit," Coram said. They stopped twenty yards away, more than enough space to detect and defend against an attack.

The figure shook its head stiffly and pointed at Rose, then again at the chair.

"Me?" Rose asked, a fearful lump building in her throat.

The figure nodded and pointed again.

Rose thought of the others suffering like this person, the refugees along the river, and the countless more to come. "We don't have time for this," she said.

Rushing forward, Meadowrue yelled, "Release the fairy!" Her face was flush, her chin jutting forward. She looked like she was about to blow.

The seated figure opened its mouth as if laughing, but nothing came out except for a dry rasp. When this spasm finally stopped—it went on uncomfortably long—it raised its hand, palm out. Then it raised the other. Its mouth twitched, its eyes shut. Suddenly, its head slammed down against the table so hard the glass canister almost toppled over.

The group eyed one another warily as the body seized. It shook as if electrocuted, arms and legs flailing. A dark liquid spilled out its mouth.

"Do we do something?" Rose asked, but no one answered. No one knew what was happening.

When the figure's body came to rest, a long minute passed. Then it raised its head again. This time its eyes were completely black.

Rose had had enough. "You're sick," she said. "Let the fairy go and maybe we can see about getting you some help," though she doubted this could be done. Something told her its illness was much too far along.

"We don't have time to waste," Rose said. "We're on our way to the Cemetery of Bad Dreams. Please, cooperate or—"

"I know exactly where you're headed, Rose Coffin."

No way that voice just came from that body. It was a deep echo, an explosion of sound that vibrated against Rose's ears. Even Orange Blossom, who had been sitting on her shoulder, jumped down and scurried behind Ridge. It was almost as if the figure was an amplifier for some demonic voice far away.

"The Abomination," Coram said, the words just barely squeezing out. "That thing is the Voice of the Abomination."

"H-how?" Rose asked, taking a small step back.

"I've heard of this happening once before. The disease, it must have made that poor soul a vessel. This person was probably just an unfortunate merchant caught in the Abomination's path. Now it's his voice."

"I commend you on acquiring the armor," the Voice said, glaring at Eo, "though I notice it cost the life of the old warrior. I should let you know his corpse is being dug up as we speak. It will be brought to me for dinner."

A wicked laugh escaped from the figure, and Eo roared in anger. He pulled forward, but Rose grabbed hold of the armor, keeping him back. She placed a hand between the Cobberjack's ears in an attempt to comfort him, but she could feel how badly he was trembling.

"More will die before you ever reach me," the Voice said. "I can promise you that. A lot more."

Rose balled her fists. *This creature is the cause of all your pain, Rose. It's the cause of countless deaths and constant suffering. It's the reason you're going to die.* Suddenly, whatever fear she had was wiped clean with anger. "We're ready to give our lives," she said. "And in turn we're going to take yours."

"With what?" the Voice asked, amused. "Those little weapons? A sword and a bow? Armor with tiny spikes? You really think they'll be enough to take me down? I grow stronger every day. Every passing hour! Soon, nothing will be able to stop me! Not even that voice of yours!" The Voice stood, a crooked stance, and pointed at Rose. "I will squeeze it from your throat." Then it sat back down, as if in pain, its entire body cracking. "Or," it said in a stretched, playful syllable. "Or you can just give it to me."

Rose laughed, shaking her head in disbelief. They all did. Even the Voice. It cackled right along with them, laughing at each one of their faces.

"I know what Queen Sequoia offered you," it finally said, its laughter snuffed out in a sharp second. "The magic she talks of, the kind that will heal your brother, it's right here." It pointed to the fairy beneath the glass. "You can have it, Rose. And it won't even cost you your life."

Suddenly, Rose's breath was stuck in her lungs. She felt as if she were choking, her entire body locking up. *What's happening here?*

"Don't listen to him, Rose," Coram said, moving close to her. "It's a trick." He sounded nervous, panicked almost.

"No trick," the Voice said. "The magic is in this ancient fairy's wings. All I have to do is use this body to rip them off and grind them into a fine powder. I will then place it into a pouch, and you will take that pouch back home to your brother, Rose. Sprinkle it over his face and the magic will take effect not long after. Not only will your brother return to your parents, but if you agree to my terms, he will also return to you. You will be together again. A family. The one you so desperately need."

"I . . . You'll let me go back?"

Everyone looked at Rose now. She had stumbled backward, a hand over her heart.

"You're not thinking of doing this, are you?" Coram asked, reaching out for her.

Rose glared at him, shoving his hands away. "And why shouldn't I? All you've ever wanted from me is my death."

"That's right," the Voice said. "They don't care about you, about what you need, your wishes and dreams." Once again, it gestured toward the empty chair. "Join me, Rose. Let us discuss this further."

Coram gazed at her as she pushed past him, his mouth open in disbelief. "Rose . . ."

This time she took the seat.

"There is no shame in wanting to live," the Voice said. "And as you so eloquently stated, what have these people ever done for you?"

"How?" Rose asked, her voice as far away as the Abomination's. "How do I give you my voice?"

"It leaves when you do. The moment you depart this world, the power in your voice will remain behind. I will consume it as I will consume everything else."

"And how do I leave?"

"Why, I will take you there myself. Or, rather, this body will."

Rose looked back at the others. They were all frozen in shock. Eo was whimpering. Ridge kept trying to speak, but nothing was coming out. Coram looked heartbroken, and Meadowrue was clearly filled with rage.

But they didn't matter right now. Not to Rose. All she could think of was how everything could finally be set right in her life. All the mistakes she'd made, all the time she'd lost with her brother. Her life could be beautiful. Her dreams could come true. After years of confusion, she knew what mattered now.

"Shall we go?" the Voice asked.

Rose hesitated. She knew she should be jumping at the opportunity, but something didn't feel right. "But . . . if I do, you'll destroy everything."

The Voice dismissed her with a wave of its hand. "What do you care of this place? When you're old, when you have children of your own, when you're an aunt to your brother's children and you're all together for the holidays, when all your dreams have been achieved, Eppersett will be nothing but a flicker of memory. You will probably question if it even existed at all. None of it will matter to you, Rose. None of it. Because you will be happy."

Rose picked up the glass case and saw her reflection in it. She didn't look like herself. Coming here to Eppersett, it turned her into someone else. Someone she had always wanted to be. She wondered if she could bring that presence back home with her.

"Yes," the Voice said. "It's all in there. The answer to all your troubles."

Rose's image in the glass faded and she could now see the fairy within. Its hands were pressed against the glass, its wings fluttering as it stared back at Rose. Meadowrue had told her about these kinds of fairies when Rose said she thought all fairies were this size. It turned out the tiny ones had mostly died off. The few that were left were quite old, and quite magical. And this one would return Rose's brother to her.

Rose's hand traced the glass, her thoughts a whirlwind. Why didn't she just agree already? What was holding her back? Turning in her seat, she glanced back at the others again. What would they do in her situation? Quite instantly, she realized they could never be in her situation because they weren't sacrificing themselves to get something in return.

They were risking death to make the world a better place and that was it. To save others, not themselves. They were true heroes.

Rose raised the glass, meeting the fairy eye to eye. Her hands were shaking.

"Do we have a deal?" the Voice asked.

Rose looked at the Voice. She looked deep into its black eyes. She didn't want to see through the diseased darkness and into the eyes of the possessed; she wanted to see straight through to the Abomination. And for a brief moment, she did. She saw it. At the other end of the darkness, she saw the monster. The whites of its eyes. And it was to those eyes she said, "No." Rising to her feet, she broke the glass against the table, the fairy taking off into the blue sky.

The Voice let out a horrid wail, overthrowing the table with a swipe of its hands. It lunged at Rose, tackling her to the ground. "Then you will die!" it said, inches from her face. "You will die before you ever reach me!" With black drool dripping from beneath each tooth, its hands gripped Rose's throat and began to squeeze. Her mouth flew open, gasping for air, and as it did she felt something touch the back of her throat, a horrible taste on her tongue. All around her she heard shouting. Seconds later, there was a struggle and the grip around her neck loosened. When she opened her eyes again, Coram was at her side, his sword through the Voice's chest.

"You . . . you had me worried there," he said.

Grasping at her throat, Rose got to her feet. The Order was all around her, concerned looks on all their faces. But not just concern; it was something deeper. She was ashamed for even thinking of abandoning them. "Are you okay?" Coram asked. "Did it hurt you?"

Though her throat burned, she shook her head. They had a mission to accomplish, and she couldn't allow anything to slow them down. "I'm fine."

Then, looking at each of them, she said, "I'm not going to run. I'm a fighter. And I fight for my brother. I fight for Eppersett."

Chapter 22
THE CEMETERY
OF BAD DREAMS, PART ONE

The closer they got to the cemetery in search of Millenten's bow and arrows, the quieter Meadowrue grew, the slower she walked, the tenser she became. In fact, the tension among all of them was palpable. Rose could feel it squeezing her entire body, her skin tightening around every bone. The air grew colder, and the sun retreated in haste. Vegetation died; animals scattered. It was as if the Abomination had already arrived.

And maybe a part of it had. The Voice hadn't left her head since the encounter. It was in there now with her own inner voice, threatening her, warning her not to continue, whispering that there was still time to save herself. Sometimes she thought she could feel it running through her mind, rifling through her memories. It kept finding her brother. She feared it might never leave.

At several points in the journey toward the cemetery, Coram had to stop and ask Meadowrue which direction to take, and her response was always given with great reluctance, a simple nod west or south, her eyes deadened.

"You've never been here before," Rose said to Coram, sidling up to him, speaking quietly. She remembered how Coram never dreamed, good or bad.

Eo, wearing the spiked armor and walking very close to Rose, as was his new habit, turned to Meadowrue, who was lagging far behind. "Um, Millenten was a fairy like you, right?"

Meadowrue gave a stiff nod; if there was pride in this relation, she was never going to show it.

"The fiercest one of them all," Ridge added. "No fear in Millenten, they say! Crazed little fairy! Lived to fight, he did! He was so skilled with the bow and arrow that legend has it he could split a Panatoo from over a thousand feet! He even predicted exactly where the little bugger would be penetrated! Eye, nose, mouth! Wherever he wished!" He looked at Orange Blossom, its face burrowing deep into Rose's shoulder. "Sorry, friend! That was a different time! You understand!"

Rose's face was scrunched up in puzzlement. "But that makes *Millenten* special, not the bow."

"Oh, Millenten was special, all right! So special that he once saved the wizard Redscale from a clan of Cyclopes! The ones with three arms, not four—the four-armed Cyclopes are just lovely! Anyway, as thanks, Redscale placed a spell on Millenten's bow and arrows, one of the strongest ever performed! Suddenly, that shot Millenten made at a thousand feet could be doubled! Tripled! His arrows could bend and curve, turn corners, stop and pick up again! Each shot traveled so fast you could hardly even see it! An incredible weapon!" Ridge always enjoyed talking about the legends of others. It was clear how much he respected these stories and the figures at the center of them. The way he spoke, it was as if he yearned to be a part of them, whispered among the trees for all time.

"And it's buried somewhere in the cemetery?" Rose said, eyebrows raised.

"That's right! Millenten always said he'd never be done fighting! 'Bury me in the Cemetery of Bad Dreams,' he said! Can you imagine?"

"But let me get this straight, we don't know where, exactly, in this miles-long cemetery of unmarked graves he lies."

"Not in the slightest!"

"So, we have to dig," she said, acknowledging the shovels Coram had purchased on Lemonwyll Bridge that were now strapped to Ridge's back. "But when we do, we'll be digging up other people's nightmares."

"Correct!"

Rose stopped. "And that doesn't sound crazy to you?"

"It does!"

Glancing back, Rose couldn't help but notice Meadowrue stumble. She looked weak, sick to her stomach. It was obvious to everyone, and all conversation dissipated not long after.

An hour later, with the sun gone for the night, the air began to fog over. Within minutes, Rose's visibility diminished to a radius of five feet, Orange Blossom but a small beacon in that fallen cloud. The group's pace slowed considerably; everyone was on edge, and the cemetery was near.

Eventually, Rose could make out the branches of a tree through the fog; they were like thick arms embracing the sky. Her neck stretched as she tried to take it all in, but she had to keep stepping back to glimpse it in full. It was an enormous tree, and for a moment, Rose thought that was why Ridge had gasped. But then, as he approached it, his hand reached out and touched the dead trunk in a soft, loving way. His head bowed. There were tears in his eyes, stifled sobs. A moment later, Ridge dropped to his knees.

The tree's roots spread around them like the tentacles of an octopus. They were largely out of the ground, twisting and turning, diving and rising. They went on and on, Rose's eyes following each one until she lost them in the fog. The tree was all gnarled and twisted and dead. No leaves, the branches naked and dry.

"It's a skeleton tree," Coram whispered to Rose. "It's all that's left of Ridge's great-grandfather, Theebius. When he died, instead of going to the Dead Forest, his wish was to be placed here to keep the bad dreams from escaping. His spirit watches over the cemetery, protecting us all from the return of our greatest fears." He pointed to the hundreds of objects at the tree's roots—carvings, food, money. "People leave him gifts whenever they come. Little offerings to show their thanks. Theebius is a legend among legends."

Stepping closer, holding Orange Blossom aloft, Rose could see the shape of the Willapp in the skeleton, the outline of his arms and legs, the contours of his face, all of it frozen in time. *He must have been massive*, she thought. Twice the size of Ridge. She reached up and snapped off her necklace, a gift from her father in what now felt like a previous life. Kneeling beside Ridge, she placed it among the other offerings. *Even in death they continue to fight*, she thought, awed.

"Does this mean we've arrived?" she asked Coram when she rose back to her feet. "Is the cemetery near?"

Coram nodded. "Just beyond Theebius."

The air was ice-cold, the moonlight lost in the fog. There wasn't a sound for miles.

Rose crept forward until the beginning of the cemetery could be made out. It was just down a short slope, the land stretching out. From what she could see, it was clear the ground was loose, as if there were fresh burials every day. Either that, or something beneath the soil was fighting to get out.

Ridge finished paying his respects, repeatedly wiping at his eyes as he stood. Still, he couldn't pull himself away from the skeleton tree. He kept talking to it, the quietest Rose had ever heard him speak. "Guide me, Theebius. Guide me to my destiny. Let my life be worth speaking of."

Eo took the lead down toward the cemetery, his armor glowing in the fog like the sun peeking through. There was a newfound sense of confidence in the Cobberjack. All fear had left him. It turned out he was his father's son after all, Rose thought.

When they reached the bottom of the slope, Ridge gave each one of them a shovel. Eo found a rock nearby and began sharpening his claws.

"We don't know what's going to come up," Coram said. "So be careful. Don't dig too recklessly."

There has to be a better way, Rose kept thinking. *There has to.*

Nobody wanted to make the first move. They each looked from one to the other, shovels in their hands.

"Perhaps it's best if we spread out," Meadowrue said, her voice like ice. It was clear how badly her hands were shaking. Everyone noticed it, but before something could be said, she dashed off into the fog, far from the others.

Rose made sure to follow. She thought nobody should be forced to face their nightmares alone.

Nearly eighty yards in, Meadowrue arched her back and was about to thrust the shovel into the ground when she froze. The shovel just hung there in midair. Looking back at Rose, her arms locked, she said, "I can't do it."

Rose was taken aback by her vulnerability. *This is a girl with ghosts*, she thought. *This is a girl with nightmares you could never imagine, Rose. This is worse than a brother in a coma. Worse than a thousand SallyAnns.* "You don't have to," Rose said. "We'll do it."

But Meadowrue shook her head. "I can't let my demons chase you. They're mine to face."

The look in Meadowrue's eyes cracked Rose's voice wide

open. Fear vibrated along each syllable. "How many of your dreams are buried here?" she asked.

Meadowrue's face went slack, the blood draining quickly. When she spoke, her chin quivered. "Hundreds. And they're all the same."

CHAPTER 23
THE CEMETERY
OF BAD DREAMS, PART TWO

The wind was fierce in the middle of the cemetery. It threw the fog from east to west so viciously that Rose's surroundings could only be glimpsed in fragments. Hidden, then uncovered, then hidden again. The effect made everything appear even more surreal than it already was. Rose would see her friends for seconds at a time—unnerved gravediggers—before they were once again lost in the never-ending fog. Like the moon behind passing clouds.

"Deedubs wasn't the only one to ever go into Widcrook," Meadowrue said, her voice hushed and distant. "I went too."

Rose lowered her shovel and walked closer. She didn't need

to ask what happened; she just put her hand on Meadowrue's back.

"It was long ago, when I still had wings. I flew all the way across the Zo, at one of its widest points, toward the north. By myself. Fairies aren't meant to fly for very long stretches, but I was always reckless like that. I was curious too, always wanted to see what was on the other side of the river. What had everyone so scared? What was so terrible about Widcrook? It turned out there was a lot. On the shores of the Zo, there was this race of creatures; they're called Kesps. They're really horrible looking—I can't even begin to describe them. Even if I could, I wouldn't want to. I see them enough in my dreams. But on that day I saw how they were being treated. They were enslaved by these tiny gremlins, Vyntills. It was brutal. The Vyntills poked and prodded them, put saddles on their backs. They beat them, kept parents from children. Worked them near death. I . . . I couldn't take it. I'd never been so incensed. I returned home that night and told everyone about it. Every fairy in Stammandy. I told them that I wanted to go back with a boat and rescue every single one of them. The elders warned me against it—I was forbidden. But I didn't care. I knew what was right. I knew what had to be done, and I shamed them all for not seeing it. Two days later, I went without permission. I put all the money I had into buying a boat, and I sailed it across the Zo by myself. In the thick of the night, I rescued as many Kesps as I could, loading them onto the boat before I was detected. I knew if we stayed to fight—if I tried to rescue everyone—we would all die. And so we fled, escaping by the skin of our teeth—myself and twenty-eight Kesps. I know it was hard for them, leaving their loved ones behind, and I promised I'd come back for the rest. Most of the Kesps with me were young; they were scared and they were angry. Well, not as angry as the fairies were when we returned to Stammandy. You see, fairies are all about beauty and nature, about family and one's own kind. They weren't open to the Kesps. They didn't see the good in them that I saw. They only saw ugliness. Filth. They considered every Kesp to be ill-mannered and ignorant. Animals. And they said it was only a matter of time before they brought violence. Needless to say, the Kesps were treated poorly. Nobody wanted them there. The fairies said their presence ruined their home, ruined everything it stood for. The Kesps weren't treated any better here than where they had come from. Then one night something horrible happened. There was a fight, an argument, and by morning the Kesps had massacred dozens of fairies. Elders, children—there was no pity. Eventually we were able to drive them out, but the blame fell on my shoulders. My wings were taken from me and

I was cast out. 'You're not a fairy anymore,' they told me. And I don't blame them. I alone was responsible for those deaths. Every single one. They're all on me. And I've been haunted by it ever since."

"But . . . you didn't know," Rose said. "You were trying to do the right thing."

"If it was right, how'd it end up so wrong?" Her lips were trembling. Her eyes blinked repeatedly.

"Because . . . because fairies were scared of something they didn't understand. They didn't share your love. Your dreams."

"I have no dreams, Rose. I have only nightmares, and they're all buried at our feet. I'm . . . I'm scared to dig them up."

Freezing, and with the wind's howl filling her ears, Rose said, "Then I will. We'll face your nightmares together."

She figured the spot where she stood was just as good as any in which to dig. *The quicker you start, the quicker it ends*, she told herself. With Meadowrue still frozen in place beside her, her arms limp at her sides, Rose plunged her shovel into the ground and drew back some dirt that was filled with writhing white worms as thick as her fingers. The deeper she dug, the thicker they got. About two feet down, where they were the size of her wrists, she hit something. A dull thwack. And it wasn't a worm. She pulled the shovel back and the dirt shifted, and she saw an eye staring up at her. It was large and yellow and filled with bubbling pus, and when it blinked, Rose let out a shriek. Quickly, she threw the dirt back over it, her heart pounding. Reality was terrifying enough in this world; she couldn't imagine what everyone's nightmares might be like.

She glanced back at Meadowrue. She was still in the same spot, still unable to move. It was as if invisible hands had risen up and grabbed hold of her ankles. After watching Rose's first attempt, she seemed to be talking to herself, psyching herself up. But whatever she said, it wasn't working. She couldn't get her body to move.

Somewhere far away, through the windblown fog, Rose heard shouts. Someone had dug up something big and a fight was taking place, though she had no clue where. It sounded horrific, a clash of weapons and gasps for help and strength. If they didn't find the bow soon, dreams wouldn't be the only things buried here.

She looked down at her shovel in frustration. *This isn't working*, she thought. *It's a needle in a haystack. If we keep digging aimlessly, we're just going to uncover more and more nightmares.*

Then, deep in her head, it was as if she could hear the Abomination laughing. The Voice was still with her, and it seemed to be growing stronger.

Behind her Meadowrue shrieked. She must have started digging while Rose was distracted. She was stumbling backward, dropping her shovel in terror, hands covering her mouth as if to keep something in.

"What is it?" Rose asked, screaming over the wind and through the fog.

"H-how?" Meadowrue said, stammering. "How is . . . how is this p-possible?"

"Rue, what is it?" she said, rushing over. "What happened?"

"The first grave . . . The very first grave I dig and . . . and . . . it's one of mine!"

Rose reached her, grabbing hold of her arm. It was ice-cold, the skin covered in goose bumps. Meadowrue's eyes—growing larger by the second—were locked on the shifting earth no more than six feet away.

Rose looked too, her stomach plummeting straight into the ground with the nightmares. Something was clawing its way to the surface, the dirt falling off it in large chunks. It was a nightmare that even the fog kept clear of.

"One of mine!" Meadowrue shouted again, shaking her head in disbelief. "It's one of mine!"

The cloaked figure rose to an imposing height. Its pointed face, horselike and skeletal, darted out of the hood. There was just the slightest amount of skin over it, thin strands about to snap. Every tooth was exposed, and there were barren holes where its nose and eyes should be. Its emaciated body was wrapped tightly beneath the raggedy cloak, worms writhing all over it.

"What is that?" Rose asked. For all the fear that swept through her body right now, she knew it was only a fraction of what Meadowrue was feeling.

Meadowrue backed away. Her swords weren't even raised— she had drawn them, but they were down at her sides. Her head shook from side to side as she cried out, "It's a Kesp. A Kesp!"

The creature shambled forward, head bobbing, a strange gasp coming from its snout. Something told Rose her voice wasn't going to work on it. Was this true? Or was it the Abomination speaking? "We're going to have to fight, Rue!"

But Meadowrue just stood there, and suddenly the Kesp was rushing toward her, head down, its cloak flowing like a cape. As Rose braced herself, it ran right by her and rammed Meadowrue in the chest, knocking her back almost a dozen feet, swords flying.

Meadowrue didn't seem hurt, but she didn't get to her feet either. There was no fight in her.

"Get up!" Rose said. "It wants you! You have to fight!"

But still, Meadowrue refused to act. She looked as if the

blow had cracked her chest open, yet, as the Kesp moved in again, she had the strength to scream.

She's just going to let it kill her, Rose thought. *It's almost as if she wants it to.*

Rose ran faster than she ever had, blinking in and out of the fog, a race with a nightmare. She reached Meadowrue just moments before the Kesp, and dived, grabbing one of the fallen swords. But by the time she turned around, the Kesp was on her, shrieking into the wind, one howl mixed with another. With her eyes closed, Rose swiped the sword through the air, connecting with the creature. She felt something give beneath the cloak, and the Kesp toppled to the side.

"Get up," Rose said to Meadowrue, trying to pull her to her feet before the monster gathered itself. "Get up!" But Meadowrue refused to budge. It was like she weighed five times her weight.

When the Kesp stood again, it ripped its cloak off and unfolding from within were the two longest arms Rose had ever seen. They just stretched and stretched, thin and sinewy. Sharp claws unfolded from the ends, fingers with several knuckles each, bending in impossible ways. Its legs unfolded too, flexing in three different places, giving the Kesp another six feet in height.

Its mouth opened wide enough to swallow Rose whole, letting out a hideous squawk, strands of flesh snapping across its expanding chest. With a long finger, it pointed at Meadowrue.

"It wants me," Meadowrue cried. "It never stops!"

Rose, her chest heaving, jumped in front of her supine friend, the sword vibrating in her hand. She tried to steady it with two hands, but that just made it worse.

"It wants me!" Meadowrue screamed again. "Move, Rose! It wants me!"

But Rose refused to budge, even as the Kesp charged. It moved so much quicker now, dropping to four legs in a wild rush. Rose barely had a second to register what was even happening. There was no time to use her voice, no time to cry out for help. Her only instinct was to raise the sword, her elbows wobbling. The Kesp leapt at them, and Rose ducked, eyes averted, as she raised her weapon toward the creature. She could feel the blade meet the stretched-out flesh, the Kesp's momentum carrying its body forward, dragging against the steel. It collapsed in a heap beside them. Writhing in agony, still reaching out, the Kesp clawed at them. Its long rows of teeth snapped, its body rising and falling. It glared at Meadowrue, and Meadowrue met its glare, her face wet with tears. "Leave me alone," she said. "Please leave me alone." The Kesp lunged and scratched her face, just below the eye.

Then, hands clutching its wound, the monster let out a small gasp and ceased moving.

Frantically cleaning herself off, Rose looked on in shock as the Kesp dissolved into the fog, not living, not dead, not even a dream anymore. She rose to her feet and felt something wiggle down her shirt. Just as she was about to scream, Orange Blossom climbed through the collar and threw half a worm to the ground.

Rose helped Meadowrue up, applying pressure to her facial wound. Blood seeped from the gash and dripped down her fingers. She couldn't believe she thought it, but she needed Meadowrue to be tougher. Next time the wound might be fatal.

"If you refuse to fight, your fears will win," she told her.

"I've survived this long, Rose."

"Is that what you call it?"

Rose knew she was being tough with her. She had to be. Just as Rose's mother had been tough with her. The problem was getting through. She wished her mother could see her now.

Meadowrue glanced down in shame. She brought her hand to her cheek and placed it over Rose's. "I have no idea how many times I've been here, Rose. Too many by far. There's going to be one of those things for each of my people killed. I . . . I can't do it. I can't face them."

"You—"

There was a scream, and Rose's head snapped toward the sound. She saw Ridge angrily charging through the fog toward a twelve-foot-tall spider. His birds had all been caught in a web, their bodies limp. Ridge's branches tangled with the arachnid's legs, each one trying to puncture the other. Just past him was a ball of light, and Rose knew this was Eo. Gold sprays were flying off his back, the spiked armor hard at work. There was no sign of Coram, and Rose felt a sharp twinge of fear in her chest.

"We'll never make it like this," she said.

"We have to run," Meadowrue cried. "I'm telling you, we have to get far away from here!"

"There has to be another way, Rue. We can't run and we can't keep digging."

"Then what?"

Rose paused, and the wind continued to blow as if it had something to say. The voice was powerful, cutting through her clothes and skin and reaching deep within her. She could feel it shove aside the Abomination's voice as if it were nothing.

The message rose up through her body. It told her she could do this, that she could help end this struggle. And it told her she knew exactly how to do it. Who was talking, Rose wasn't sure. But she had a feeling it might be Eppersett itself. This strange new world reaching out to her. Straightening up, Rose closed her eyes, letting the message take hold. And then she had it. Over time, she was beginning to understand her abilities more and more. She now realized it didn't always have to be some kind of attack or defense. It could be something more subtle, like when she called Orange Blossom to her inside the labyrinth. She had the power to manipulate the world around her. If she sang now, it would be a kind of communication with the beyond. She could tap into something hidden, some astral plane. Eppersett itself. And as the song began to pass through her lips, it was as if she was asking the world to sing with her.

"But I still haven't found what I'm looking for . . ."

She sang this line over and over again, a type of pleading, a type of prayer.

"But I still haven't found what I'm looking for . . ."

Meadowrue was silent beside her, holding her face, staring in awe, as Rose was suddenly pulled forward, her back arched, as if something had yanked her heart.

Still with her eyes closed, Rose walked through the cemetery. Or was she carried? Guided? Battles were taking place all around her. The spider was gone, but there was now something like a half human, half rat. It was ten feet tall and carried an ax as it faced down Eo and Ridge. Minutes later, she strode straight between Coram and another of Meadowrue's

Kesps. Coram tried shouting at her, but Rose heard nothing but the whispered instruction in her ears to keep walking west.

After a few hundred yards, the ground rumbled, and Rose opened her eyes. About ten feet ahead of her, the earth was shifting, as if something were bubbling up from beneath.

"It's there," Rose said, breaking her trance. "The weapon, it's there. We have to dig."

Rose stuck her shovel in the ground and turned to Meadowrue, who had followed closely. "I can't do this alone. I know you're scared, but I need your help. You can do this."

Meadowrue shook her head. "There are things I can't face, Rose. I don't want to see what rises up out of there."

"Whatever it is, Rue, you face it. You face it and I promise you will never have to again, as long as you live." She reached out and grabbed Meadowrue's hand. "Fight with me."

Meadowrue's eyes watered, her lips shifting as if to contain her sobs. "Okay," she croaked. "Okay. Together." And she thrust her shovel into the ground, joining Rose.

Together, they began to dig, far deeper than Rose imagined they'd have to. Six feet down, her back began to ache, her muscles throbbing. Although it was freezing out, she was sweating. For a moment, she thought she had been led to the wrong place, that her voice, and that of Eppersett's, had failed her. Maybe it was the Abomination after all.

But then she saw a hand.

Jumping back and climbing out of the hole, Rose and Meadowrue watched as the figure slowly clawed its way to the surface.

What finally emerged was something Rose could hardly explain. Somehow, she was standing face-to-face with a second Meadowrue, Millenten's bow and arrows across her back.

Chapter 24
THE CEMETERY
OF BAD DREAMS, PART THREE

The real Meadowrue looked ready to faint. She was woozy, swaying where she stood as the word *no* escaped from her mouth over and over again, quiet at first, but growing louder with each utterance. When she began to retreat, her legs almost gave out beneath her, and she was screaming the word.

Rose too backed away. Although this creature looked like Meadowrue, it was also clearly evil, its eyes hauntingly dark. They were eyes that wished to see nothing but pain in others, suffering and heartache throughout all the world. The creature's posture was poor, as if its body had been warped by past sins, turning in on itself and discoloring, rotting from the inside out. A long, split tongue shot from its mouth like a snake, and its wings were missing like Meadowrue's, but they throbbed and oozed.

What is this? Rose wondered. *This isn't Millenten. It must be something else. Something put here to guard the bow.*

The creature headed for Meadowrue, who was now quivering so bad she dropped to her knees and buried her face in her hands.

It's going to kill her, Rose thought. *Do something!*

"Hey!" she screamed, tossing a rock at its head.

Hissing, the creature turned to Rose, and in that instant Rose saw it take on a different form. It wasn't Meadowrue anymore, but Rose's brother. Rose saw what he looked like the very last time she had ever set eyes on him in that hospital bed, tubes and scars, his body locked up but somehow walking.

Rose instantly felt weak. It was as if her heart had opened up inside her, cracking like an egg and spilling down her torso. Her bones were like ice, the blood drained from her face. She was nothing but memories now, shameful, guilt-ridden memories wrapped in fear and insecurity.

Had the creature wished, it could have killed her. But instead, it went back for Meadowrue.

Watching it come, once again in its original form, Meadowrue grabbed her sword, but her hands were shaking so badly, she immediately dropped it. She was crawling backward like a crab, saying, "No. That's not me. That's not me."

Luckily, Rose was given a reprieve. No longer faced with her brother, she was able to gather herself, if only a little. Meadowrue's other sword was still in her possession. Raising it over her head, she threw it end over end at the creature, and to her complete surprise, it went straight through its back and out its stomach. The creature howled in pain, grabbing at the blade. With fiery eyes, it turned toward its attacker and this time Rose was faced with her mother. She saw her old and hobbled and broken.

"Mom, I'm sorry." Her voice was a croak, her hands extending in sorrow. "I'm so sorry."

With the sword now free, the creature turned away and once again distorted itself into the dark Meadowrue.

It's playing off our fears, Rose thought. *It shifts to our greatest nightmares. That's its power.*

She looked at how horrified her friend was to see this altered image of herself. *This is who she fears she really is*, Rose realized. *This is how she sees herself, how she imagines others view her. All her guilt, all her shame, it turned her insides into this.*

As the creature neared, Rose called out to Meadowrue. "That's not you! Rue, that will never be you!"

"But it is," Meadowrue cried. "It is. I'm a monster."

"No. I don't see you that way, Rue. None of us do. We see someone strong. Someone kind. We see a friend."

Meadowrue glanced over at Rose. There were tears in her eyes; her chin quivered. "I messed up so bad, Rose."

"You did what you thought was right. You were trying to bridge people. It's not your fault. They were all too scared to see it."

With a tortured scream, the creature turned and rushed Rose, morphing into a deranged mixture of her mother, brother, and SallyAnn. In brutal flashes, they traded body parts—her brother's head became SallyAnn's; her mother's body became her brother's; at one point, the face was comprised of features from all of them at once. The three nightmares came for her, lurching and writhing, and only at the last second did Coram step in front and shove his sword into the monster's belly, two wounds side by side. As he removed his sword, the creature stepped back, struggling to find a form. *Coram doesn't dream*, Rose remembered. *There are no nightmares to draw from.* With nothing to haunt him with, the creature rose up as a Kesp and charged Coram, knocking the sword from his hands and barreling him in the chest.

Coram couldn't breathe. On his knees, he kept clutching at his throat, searching for the air that was knocked from him.

The Kesp moved in, swatting Rose aside as if she were nothing.

As it stood over Coram, it raised both its claws.

He winced as the monster attacked, his arms shielding his face. A strange sound cut through the fog, and Rose watched as a spray of gold spikes rushed forth, penetrating the creature's chest just before it struck Coram. The spikes ripped through the Kesp with astounding force, then snapped back to their resting place on Eo's armor.

Ridge had joined them too now, his branches wrapping around the creature and squeezing it tight.

In defense, the Kesp became a fire demon, its glow burning bright in Ridge's horrified eyes. All at once, the branches lost their grip, Ridge withering in the creature's presence. Eo, however, approached for a second strike, and the fire demon became Deedubs, snarling and mashing at his son.

Rose saw her friends' confusion and apprehension, their fear. Ridge was still recovering from what he had witnessed, and Eo was unable to fire the spikes. They both were vulnerable now, defenseless. And that was when Meadowrue leapt onto the creature's back. Suddenly, there were two Meadowrues again, one atop the other.

But to Rose, it was clear which one was which. She knew who her friend really was, and she was exhilarated when she realized Meadowrue wasn't scared anymore.

As the creature tried to shake her off, Meadowrue raised her sword. With a scream of a thousand nightmares, she drove it into her dark self's neck over and over again, until they both dropped.

On the ground, the creature held its throat, the blood spurting out from between its fingers. It glared at Meadowrue, struggling to speak.

"You can't . . . hide who you . . . are. This is . . . you. A . . . killer of fairies. A killer . . . of your kind. Unworthy of wings."

Meadowrue got to her feet and raised her sword once more. "You're right. I can't hide. And I won't. You're a part of me. One that I'm going to kill for good."

And she brought her sword down on the creature, chopping off its head.

Separated, both body and head twitched and shuffled through forms until all that was left was a pale, weak creature. A shriveled, indistinct thing. It bled out on the ground, pathetic and nothing to fear.

Exhausted, Meadowrue collapsed to her knees and wept into her hands. Rose kneeled beside her, an arm around her shoulder. She was so proud of her, and she told her so.

Meadowrue gazed up at her and tried to speak. When nothing came, Meadowrue just threw her arms around her.

Eventually, the creature was lost to the wind and the fog, leaving nothing behind but the bow and arrows. They belonged to Meadowrue now. She had earned them. Her nightmare was over.

CHAPTER 25
THE VOICE INSIDE

With two of the three weapons in their possession, they headed back east, returning to the river. The third and final weapon—the sword of Tarr—was farther south. They would find it where the Zo bent, in the Castle of Witches.

But first they would need some rest. Rose especially. She thought it was just the cemetery that made her feel weak and feverish, but those symptoms weren't going away. Almost a full day after their battle with the buried nightmares, when they reached yet another encampment along the river, her brow slick with sweat, her body shivering, she collapsed to the ground.

"I'm okay. I'm okay," she said as everyone gathered around. But she clearly wasn't, because a moment later, as she tried to get back on her feet, she passed out cold.

∗

Her mind was a dark place. A night with no stars. The inside of a coffin.

And it had the sounds to match. None. A vacuum. Nothingness.

Except for the voice.

"Rose. I found you, Rose."

It was the darkness itself calling out to her.

Rose walked hypnotically out into the pitch. There was no floor on which to set her feet. No walls. No ceiling. Just black upon black.

"Where are you?" she asked the voice, her own words sucked into the void. "I know you're near. I can feel you. But I can't see you."

"That's because you are me, Rose. And I am you. We are one." A sloshing sound accompanied the voice now. A persistent and steady surge.

"Who are you?" she asked, a tide of terror pulling at her heart.

"You know very well who I am."

"Get out of my head!"

A terrible laughter screeched through the darkness, and as if there was a tear in the black fabric of her mind, Rose saw a flicker of light. And in it she saw her friends. She saw Eppersett. It all came and went in brief and blinding flashes. And with a tremor in her very being, Rose realized why: She was inside the Abomination. It had swallowed her whole.

✳

When she came to, she found herself in a large tent. She was sopping wet and breathing heavily. It was dark, the only light coming from Orange Blossom beside her. She was on the ground, covered in thick blankets, a pillow beneath her head. Coram was standing over her, as well as someone she had never seen before.

"This is Preego," Coram said. "She was a doctor before fleeing the Abomination."

Preego leered at Coram. "I am *still* a doctor."

"Of course." Coram coughed, clearly embarrassed.

Preego was covered in orange fur, like a tiger, with bulging green eyes and long whiskers. Her tail was in the air, nearly reaching her head. She was beautiful, and Rose feared how many of her kind the Abomination had wiped out.

Just then, she felt a crack through her head at the thought of its name. Her eyes slammed shut, and she grabbed at her skull, a groan escaping her lips.

Concerned, Coram took her hand in his. "Rose, Preego has taken a look at you and . . . I'm afraid it's not good."

"Wait. Am I going to die?" Rose asked, almost laughing. "Don't tell me I'm going to die soon."

When she saw the puzzled looks on their faces, she actually did break out in laughter. It was all absurd. Since she had first come here, it had been nothing but. And after everything she had been through, she couldn't control her emotions anymore. The laughter built and built, tears streaming down her face, tears that so badly needed to flow. *What a joke*, she thought. *What an absolute joke.*

With a snap of his wrists, Coram removed the blanket covering Rose. His gaze went from her eyes to her feet and back, suggesting she take a look herself.

Glancing down at her feet, Rose noticed they were bare. Curious, she wiggled her toes. There was something off with them, but in her haze and in the dim light, she had trouble placing it. The laughter continued, but only in her head now. It didn't even sound like her own anymore, a depraved humor that frightened her.

Suddenly, she knew what the problem was. Her feet were covered in white.

Lurching to a sitting position, her eyes shot toward Coram. "I'm . . . I'm infected," she said, recalling how her throat burned as the Voice drooled black liquid over her gasping mouth.

"Abomination's disease," Preego confirmed.

"That's why I can hear its voice." Gazing off, she said this as if speaking to herself.

Preego and Coram glanced at each other warily. "You can hear it?" Preego asked.

Rose closed her eyes, returning to the darkness of her dream. The voice was there, its mind. Suddenly, it was as if she had linked with it. "It knows we're coming. It knows there's only one weapon left. It's picking up speed, gaining as much strength as possible."

"We have to move, then," Coram said.

"She can't go," Preego told him. "It's spreading, and fast."

Rose picked up Orange Blossom, who was in a tight ball on her pillow. "All the more reason, then."

Preego placed a hand on her shoulder. "I've seen this disease many times. It is going to drain you quickly. You'll have little strength. Then, when you're at your weakest, it's going to overtake your mind. Seize control of your movements, your actions. I'm sorry, but your time is short."

"My time's been short ever since I got here." She jumped down from the bed and nearly lost her balance. There was laughter in her head. This time it clearly wasn't hers.

Rose bent down and grabbed her shoes, putting them on. "Where are the others?"

"Waiting on you," Coram said.

They think you're a leader. Rose wasn't even sure whose voice she was hearing anymore. She placed her hands against her temples, scrunching her face in pain.

"The south is destroyed," Preego said. "There's nothing left. My home . . ." Her mouth moved, but nothing came out. She stammered, her eyes filling; then she turned away as they spilled. "It's terrible. There's no mercy in that thing. It comes for everything and everyone. Beautiful lands full of green, full of riverbeds and trees, hills and fields of crops. Flowers and art, unbelievable architecture, centuries of history. All of it destroyed. Like nothing had ever been there. Like we had never been there. I saw children thrown hundreds of feet through the air. I saw elderly men and women impaled by flying debris. Those that refuse to budge, they wither like the land. The Abomination is the end as we know it. It's moving fast now. Speeding death."

"The Castle of Witches, does it still stand?" Coram asked, his hands on Preego's shoulders.

Preego nodded. "I don't know for how much longer. But that place is just death inside more death. The witches probably revel in all this destruction. They welcome the end."

"We don't have any other choice," Rose said. "How far is it?" she asked Coram.

"The castle? By foot? Two weeks. Three, maybe."

"She can't make that journey," Preego said, nodding at Rose. "And the Abomination will reach you before you ever get there."

Rose walked past them and unzipped the tent. The river filled the view. "Then we get a boat."

Chapter 26
JOURNEY BY BOAT

The refugees along the river pitched in with everything they had to help the Order get a boat. They dug into their pockets, riffled through their belongings, handed over long-held valuables and jewels; they even took the clothes right off their backs. It was one of the most beautiful things Rose had ever seen. Each one of them had little of their own, but they sacrificed it all in the hopes that the Abomination would be stopped.

The boat was a piece of junk—a barely-held-together rust bucket of a thing with the color of a pig after rolling in mud for the day—but it would get them where they needed to go. It smelled like rotten vegetables boiling in sewage, and there were numerous critters living in the cracks and holes that Eo and Orange Blossom tried to sniff out but couldn't come to kill. They tossed whatever they could overboard, the haggard elf they had hired to drive the boat deeming that the little varmints had no problem swimming, though Rose wasn't sure—the elf, who was named Bendi and had but one eye, looked like he couldn't care less about anything outside himself and money. It was enough to drive Rose belowdecks, where she spent most of the trip, usually in bed getting as much rest as possible. By now the white of the disease was up past her knees and spreading quickly, the voice growing louder in her head, taunting her, threatening her. It said she would never succeed, that she would never even reach the sword. Worst of all was that she was starting to believe it.

Someone was constantly by her side to keep her company, even if she was sleeping. If she was awake, she was above deck, where they all huddled around as if she were a fire keeping them warm. Which was funny because she did feel like she was burning up, even as temperatures were dropping.

There was a constant somber air about the group, the conversation failing to remain upbeat no matter how many songs Ridge sang. He sang one for each bird he lost; they all had names apparently, and at the moment, he had gotten through twenty-one out of the fifty-six that had lived in his branches, now unnervingly barren. There was a lot of pacing too, a lot of blank stares, and much dread. And then there was Meadowrue.

"When we're at the end of this journey," she said to the group, "if we fail or if we fall, the Abomination looming over us, what will you most regret?"

Everyone grew even quieter than they already were. It was quite the question, but Rose knew her answer right away: How she ran. How she always ran.

But she didn't want to say that. She didn't want the pity or anyone telling her she was wrong, that she did the best she could. Because she didn't. She had succumbed to the pain of her life, and that wasn't acceptable.

And so she said her one other regret in life. "I wish I would have stood up to SallyAnn. Just once."

"Um, who is SallyAnn, and stuft?"

"A horrible person with a stupid face," Coram said.

"Oh, I hate horrible people!" Ridge said. "Tell us, Rose! Feed my hate for this person with the stupid face!"

"I don't know," Rose said, suddenly wishing she hadn't brought it up. "It's not that simple. I mean, I guess on the surface it is. She acts like she's better than everyone else. Her jokes are mean-spirited. She's superficial. Anyone can tell she only cares about herself. I . . . I don't like the way she makes me feel about myself."

"What kind of a warrior is she?" Ridge asked. "A barbarian? A thief?"

"Well, she's not exactly a warrior at all. I mean—how can I explain this better . . . ?" She thought a moment. "She seems like a villain, right? I mean, she made me cry myself to sleep. She made me scared to go to school. But when it comes down to it, I think SallyAnn might be in a lot of pain."

"I'll show her pain!" Ridge said.

"Me too," Meadowrue said. "I wish I could have faced SallyAnn in combat."

"That's my regret too," Coram added.

"And mine," Eo said.

Rose looked at all of them, and her smile grew. She knew they would fight for her; they wouldn't question it for a second. It warmed her more than the fever ever could. It warmed her inside and out. And it was then that Rose realized what her second regret would really be: having to leave her friends.

✳

The farther south they traveled, the worse the weather became. Day after day, the wind picked up, the skies grayed, and the boat rocked more and more. Eventually, Rose got sick and threw up, but the event barely registered on her radar. Instead, she focused on the masses of people who could be seen fleeing their homeland. The numbers grew and grew, stretching far into the horizon.

"What's happening?" she asked. In the distance, from where the refugees fled, everything looked dead. There was no color. The trees were bare, the grass brown. The smaller tributaries of the Zo were all dried up. It was a storm of a world.

Coram gripped the side of the boat, his entire body tense. "The Abomination. It's getting closer."

Rose closed her eyes for a moment and found that hidden presence within her. She hated going there. It was like falling through ice. Suddenly, her eyes sprang back open with great clarity. "It knows that with the weapons we're a threat. There's fear there, I can feel it. It doesn't want to wait to face us anymore. It's making a charge for the Castle of Witches as we speak. It wants to stop us from finding the sword. If it does that, it wins."

"It must not be far off now."

"How much longer until we reach the castle?" Rose asked.

"Another day," Coram said. "Two at most. I think we can reach it before the Abomination does. It sits in the middle of the river, right at the bend. It's like a bridge between Eppersett and Widcrook."

"Um, I can smell its foul stench from here, and stuft," Eo said, nose raised.

"The witches like to infect both lands with their ills," Coram said. "They take great pleasure in it."

"Will they have fled?" Rose asked in hope, but Coram shook his head. "No. They fear nothing. Not the Abomination. Not the end. To them, it's all the same."

Rose felt faint and crashed back against the boat.

"Are you okay?" Coram asked, taking her by the hand.

"Yeah. It's . . . it's just the boat. Hard to keep balance in these waters."

"The Abomination is near, Rose. You have to conserve your energy. Whatever happens in that castle, don't use your voice. You'll need every bit of strength for what comes after."

"I said I'm okay."

But that was a lie, of course. In reality, the disease was spreading fast, and she felt very weak. Her muscles and bones ached; she felt numb, like her body no longer belonged solely to her. Since she had been infected, a great fear had been welling up deep within her and it was horrifying. The kind of fear that consumed a person—that's how it made her feel, eaten away. When the disease eventually reached her throat— and it would very soon (she feared—no, she knew)—it would attack the only weapon she had against the Abomination. It would attack and it would win. And how could she ever save her brother if she didn't have her voice?

CHAPTER 27
THE CASTLE OF
WITCHES, PART ONE

The castle was more like a pyramid. One that was upside down, its point thrust deep into the river. By Rose's estimate, it must have stood close to a thousand feet into the sky, black and smooth, a triangular rip in space. There was no shine to it, no reflection. Any light that reached it died a quick death.

Apparently, there were several myths about the castle's creation. Or more accurately, about its arrival. It was said by many that one day it wasn't there, and the next day it was. This had happened over several thousand years ago, and Rose understood that there might have been some exaggeration or alterations to the story over that time. It was tough to sort through it all and come away with some kind of truth. Often, the answer was something in between the details. While some said the castle fell from the sky, like a dagger driving deep into the river, others were convinced it just blinked into existence, like some incredible magic. Stranger still, others maintained that, even now, it didn't exist at all, that it was nothing more than an illusion. There were rumors of doors sliding open near the very top of the castle late at night and witches and other objects flying out. Some believed that the castle poisoned the river or that the witches were the reason Widcrook had fallen into chaos and darkness. Some said the castle was sinking inch by inch every year, while others maintained that there were scores of other pyramids just like this one beyond the mountains, and soon all those witches would cross over to Eppersett, wiping out everyone. That was if the Abomination didn't get them first.

Whatever its origins, whatever its mysteries, Rose knew the castle was their final stop before facing their destiny. It didn't matter where the witches came from or what they had planned. What mattered was that they held the sword of Tarr.

A mile from the castle, the boat stopped dead in the water. Bendi refused to take them any closer, stating he was crazy but not *that* crazy. Instead, he docked the boat along the river's edge and forced everyone to depart. Then, seconds after their feet hit the ground, he had the boat turning around and heading back upriver, the water chopping at its hull.

The winds were incredible—eighty miles per hour and gaining fast. Rain fell with a force like nothing Rose had ever experienced, spiking the top of her head and soaking her clothes. Her feet were buried to her ankles, the ground one big mud trap sucking at her shoes. This, compounded with her illness, made her wonder if she were dead already. Trees fell as if a giant pushed them over, and Ridge winced with each crack of their trunks. Rose kept expecting to see the Abomination come rushing out of the gray horizon at any moment. But that wasn't so. It seemed they had reached the castle before it had, and that meant they still had a chance. But if they didn't find the sword soon, they might be trapped inside the castle when it did arrive, and that would spell trouble.

There were two narrow bridges leading to the castle, one from either side of the river. They must have usually sat well above the water, but now with the Abomination's storm, the river raised fast, flooding the bridges. The Order had to cross slowly, the winds pushing against them as if to keep them back. As the sky rumbled overhead, Rose put her head down and strode forward, her face whipped by lashes of rain and sharp gusts of wind. Orange Blossom was tucked in a ball beneath her shirt, shivering and glowing like some neon heart. To the south, the storm clouds looked even worse, and they were moving in fast. It was a nightmarish sky filled with lightning and darkness. A hurricane sky.

When they reached the door of the castle, they quickly huddled behind it, dripping wet and shivering, as they discussed their next step.

"Can we draw them outside?" Rose asked, her voice strained with sickness.

By the way Coram's brow crinkled, Rose could tell he was clearly confused. "What? Why?"

"Water is a weakness for them?" Rose said, and what began as a statement ended as a question, her voice high in uncertainty, as everyone else's face gradually began to mirror Coram's. "Isn't it?"

"Let me guess," Coram said. "You got this from those screens of yours?"

"Well, yeah. Witches, they melt or something. They can't swim."

Coram was staring at her, dumbfounded, quietly repeating her words. "Melt or something. Can't swim."

"No?" She felt sick. Maybe she wasn't thinking straight. Maybe such an idea was planted in her head by the Abomination. She wished she was home in bed. Warm. Safe.

"If that were the case, why would they build their castle atop a river?"

"I don't know. All I know is that you said there are hundreds of them in there," Rose said, pointing with a trembling finger. "And if that's true, we need a weapon."

"Do you think I don't know that? That I'm not prepared?" Coram threw down his bag and began to rummage through it. "Cortid Tarr was a witch-hunter, Rose. That was his life mission. Any witches that were foolish enough to wander outside the castle, he hunted down and slayed. Single-handedly. But one thing he never did? He never entered the castle. That, he realized, would be suicidal. There were just too many for one man to take down."

"Great," Rose said. "Way to build confidence."

Coram raised a finger, his head still in the bag. "However, after decades of battling them, he finally discovered their weakness, which is why he created the flaming sword of Tarr." He pulled out four torches and handed one to each of them—Eo, of course, going without. "Fire," he said. "That's what melts them. The opposite of water. I swear, these screens of yours are going to be your world's downfall."

"So, four torches. That's what we've got." She wanted to cry.

"Any better ideas?"

Rose sighed and extended her torch, her hand visibly shaking. "Just light me already."

"Can we get the door open first so that these don't burn out?"

Rose glanced up to the gray sheet of sky. "Right." Backing away, she waved them onward. She felt like she was about to black out. "It's probably locked, I'm guessing."

Everyone gave Eo some room as his armor began to glow. In seconds, the spikes rose up and plowed into the door with devastating force. Once they penetrated, they then quickly retreated, recoiling on their golden cords, the door splintering into sharp metallic shards. With force like that, Rose realized they would be inside within minutes. Though that was still more than enough time for fear to settle in. In fact, it was enough time for it to build a permanent home. She braced herself against the wall, her legs weak. *Rose, you've made it this far, but how much farther can you go? You weren't built for this. This is bigger than you.*

The spikes were fired again and again until nothing was left but a large, deep hole. A dark mouth into which they stared.

"Now," Coram said, grinning at Rose, "I can light your torch."

The inside of the castle was completely black, the walls sleek and severe, angling down at strange angles, allowing for little room to navigate. It was a claustrophobic darkness, but every now and then, there would be a gleam running along the walls, like trapped lightning. The inside was alive in ways the outside wasn't, and it terrified Rose. Her nerves quickly overwhelmed her senses, squeezing her body tight. A deep-seated fear banged against her bones looking for a way out.

"So, what happened to Cortid Tarr, then?" she asked, wiping at her damp brow.

They were speaking in whispers now, Coram leaning close, a torch in one hand, a sword in the other. "Well, yes, Tarr did have the sword, but by that time in his life, he was a bit crazy in the head—the effect of absorbing one too many spells. One stormy evening, he charged in here, mowing them down one by one. Who knows how many he slayed—there were rumors it was well over a hundred. Supposedly he made it all the way to the top of the castle before he was finally overwhelmed, sword or no sword. Days later, his body was found floating in the river. I'm not even going to get into what he looked like. Not while we're in here. Anyway, the witches have kept the sword to make sure it doesn't fall into anyone else's hands. Most likely, it's being kept at the top of this place. So that's where we'll go."

"Wait. Tarr was a witch-hunter with a lifetime of experience. If he was crazy, what's that make us?"

"Just north of crazy!" Ridge said, a tad too loud, as was his habit. The words seemed to bounce off the walls, traveling all the way to the top of the castle and back. He covered his mouth with one hand and with the other rotated a finger beside his temple.

Moments later, they found a narrow staircase in what must have been the exact middle of the castle. The steps seemed to be of a material Rose had never come across before. They were smooth with sharp edges, an obsidian shine to them, and ice-cold to the touch.

As she ascended, she held the torch tight in her hands, its flame flickering with a sharp snap. The air was cold, her breath showing. She could hear the wind blowing from outside, slamming against the castle walls. There were creaks and shudders, and she feared something was about to give. She imagined the entire building coming down atop her.

Her legs were heavy, as if great weights were tied to her ankles. Her heart beat rapidly, overexerting itself to keep her on her feet. Sweat poured down her face, her temples pounding, a spiking pain behind her eyes. Her hands wouldn't stop trembling, and her insides felt as if they were about to spill out through her skin. She wasn't sure if this was the illness or the fear. In the dark, she couldn't see where the white had spread, but she could feel it inching up past her chest. She found it difficult to breath. And that was before she saw something in the shadows overhead.

Curious, she stood taller, raising the torch high. And that's when she had her first glimpse of a witch.

It hung upside down like a bat, its face as pale as a sheet of paper. It didn't have a pointed hat, as she expected, perhaps foolishly, but was bald, its head badly misshapen. Its nose was short, sunken almost to the point of nonexistence, and its mouth was a narrow slit with small but sharp teeth along with a thick black tongue. It didn't have ears, but two tiny holes on either side, and impossibly large eyes that bulged far outside its head.

It dropped down in front of them, hissing in a way that ripped the insides of Rose's ears. There was no broom between its legs, no cloak or cape upon its shoulders. The witch was skinny and short, its skin almost rotten in appearance, its rags loose-fitting and barely existent. Its bare feet didn't touch the ground. Somehow, it hovered there above the stairs, waiting for them.

Meadowrue raced forward and raised her torch. Squealing, the witch reached out its hand, its fingers long with skin dangling off the tips of each and, with a wave, ripped Meadowrue's torch right out of her hands and flung it far up the stairs. In the dark, something skittered down and snuffed the flame out.

In the blink of an eye, Meadowrue grabbed her bow and fired off an arrow. It flew right through Rose's flame, catching fire and striking the witch in the center of its chest. The flames spread quickly, engulfing the witch in seconds. In a dozen more, there was nothing left but ash.

Exhaling deeply, Coram nodded at Meadowrue. "Nice going."

"Yeah, well, if we lose any more torches, my arrows aren't going to be enough."

"That was just one witch," Rose said, a tremor in her voice. "One of hundreds."

"Not that there's been a census," Coram said. "Who knows, maybe there're fewer."

"Maybe there're more," Rose said, nearly shouting.

"Ah, yes," Ridge said. "But we have passion! We have purpose! And that burns brightest of all!"

"I hope so," Meadowrue said, pointing at the top of the stairs. "Because here comes some more."

Rose glanced up and saw a mass of witches glaring down at her. They filled the staircase, one piled atop another. They were like one large monster, their arms and legs hanging over one another in unnatural ways. Then, as one, they came screaming down at them, and all at once Rose knew their small fires wouldn't be enough.

Chapter 28
THE CASTLE OF WITCHES, PART TWO

Though there was nothing visible taking hold, Rose could feel the torch being lifted from her hand. She placed her free hand on it as well, pulling with everything she had against the unseen force, but she could feel it slipping from her grasp. Golden spikes and flaming arrows kept flying past her head and exploding before her. As she narrowed her eyes, the mass of witches erupted into a wall of fire, screaming and hissing and writhing. Dark smoke filled the stairway and a putrid stench clogged her nose, but the pull of the torch lightened. Opening her eyes, she watched as Coram charged forward, cutting into the burning witches with his sword and quickly rendering them to ash. The fire made them vulnerable, she realized, far easier to vanquish. Ridge's branches scaled the walls around her, finding the witches hiding in the darkness and pulling them into the fire.

They were winning; they were actually winning. The witches were scurrying off in retreat and, for a moment, Rose thought they might actually be able to do this.

Ridge, puffed up with pride, looked at the others, a huge grin across his face. "Not bad! Not bad at all! We'll be legends yet!"

"Don't gloat," Meadowrue said, the arrows she'd fired magically returning to her quiver. "They were testing us. They wanted to see what we're about. Next time around they're not going to be so easy."

Well, that's deflating, Rose thought. But she knew it was also most likely true. They had to be careful. There was no room to get cocky. That's how mistakes were made.

They climbed higher through the castle, the wind from outside sounding more and more threatening with each step, a turbulent howl that could have been the Abomination itself. Rose couldn't imagine what it must be like out there. It sounded like a war. Like Eppersett was being ripped from reality. There were cracks of thunder that shook the entire castle, and everyone inspected the walls carefully, as if it might fall apart any second.

"This is bad," Coram said. "The closer the Abomination gets, the worse it's going to be. We have to move fast before we're buried in here."

They quickened their pace, rising and rising through the castle and, to their relief, they didn't encounter any witches for some time. But Rose knew that wasn't exactly a good thing. There were far too many in here for them to be hiding for long. The tension mounted with each step, and she found it almost unbearable until, a few flights later, she was proven right. They had walked right into a trap.

Like ghosts, the witches came straight out of the walls. First arms and legs, then entire bodies. Without warning, they appeared right atop the Order, closing off any escape up or down the staircase. In seconds, they had engulfed Ridge, spreading through his branches, their touch paralyzing him.

"I can't move!" he screamed. "I can't move!"

The torch was pulled from his hand and snuffed before his eyes. Then they went for his throat. Rose's hands trembled as she watched their mouths growing impossibly wide, their jaws unhinging, row after row of razor-sharp teeth emerging. With a trembling hand, she raised her torch to the one nearest to her, and it quickly backed away, its eyes frozen on Rose, its tongue lashing out in her direction.

Beside her, Eo shot his spikes into the branches, piercing the witches who were climbing down from them and toward

Ridge. They writhed on the golden spikes as he pulled them free from the branches, slamming them hard against the wall. As they were pinned, Coram set them afire with his torch.

But as this happened, Rose was pulled back. There were no hands on her, but she went flying backward all the same, tumbling down the stairs. When she finally came to a stop more than a dozen steps from the others, her body was all twisted up, her legs awkwardly pinned beneath her, blood seeping from her skin. She moved, very gently, a groan escaping her lips. *Nothing's broken*, she thought. *A miracle. You're going to live. For a little while anyway.* But as she looked up, she saw three witches floating down the stairs toward her and realized it might be even sooner than she thought. They came fast, hands extended, their mouths wide open. Rose glanced around quickly, desperately. Her friends were too overwhelmed by the other witches to do anything; there was no way they'd reach her in time. Behind her, three steps down, lay her torch. The flame was small but alive.

The witches were nearly on top of her, and Rose couldn't get up; there was too much pain, her body locked tight. She tried sliding down the stairs on her back, her arm reaching out behind her for the torch. The sharp steps dug into her skin, slicing it open. She stretched as far as she could go, but the torch was just out of her reach, her fingertips nudging it however slightly. If she pushed it any more, it might go tumbling all the way down.

The witches reached her. She could feel their hands on her legs, skittering up toward her torso, where Orange Blossom hid trembling. Within seconds, they would be draining them both of life. She braced herself. She had come far, but there was no pride in such an achievement. All that mattered was reaching the Abomination and saving her brother. In the end, she had failed.

As the witches' faces hovered over her, salivating over the fresh meat, something large slammed against the castle. The entire structure shook, and the witches were thrown against the wall. A strange sensation lurched in Rose's gut as the castle began to tilt. Her hand was still open, reaching for the torch, and it rolled right into her grasp. Gripping it tight, she reached up, and thrust the flame into the trio of witches, watching them burn. Seconds later, Coram leapt through the fire. He picked Rose up and put her on his back, begging some unseen entity to keep her alive.

They were all breathing heavily now, the castle straining to stand. Only Rose still had a torch—Coram must have lost his sometime in the melee. All around them, the light was dimming and the storm was raging.

After gathering themselves, they continued climbing, the stairwell vertiginously tilted. They walked on an angle, and although a few witches kept appearing out of nowhere every now and again, there wasn't a second large coordinated attack. For that, Rose was thankful. She was well enough to walk now, but she ached all over, her body sick with fever. Still, she had to push through; they were so close now.

"They're not hiding," Meadowrue said. "And they're not scared."

"They're waiting," Rose agreed. She knew it to be true, and the thought alone was enough to nearly fell her.

Eventually, they reached the end of the stairs. They were at the very top of the castle. There was a long dark hall before them, and at the end of it was a red door.

"The sword," Coram said. "It has to be in there."

Nothing stirred in the hall. It was empty, the walls tilted and blank, begging their trespass.

"It's another trap," Meadowrue said.

There was a second crash against the castle, and it wobbled some more, a deep screech running throughout from the bowels all the way to the top. Cracks could be heard spreading along the walls, the wind incredibly intense. It was like there was a perpetual shock wave slamming into the castle.

"Well, we can't just sit here and wait," Coram said. "We have to run for it."

They all looked at one another, their faces grave. Rose

nodded, and soon they all nodded in return. Then, with deep breaths, they took off.

A few strides into their run, and Rose really thought they were actually going to make it. The door was getting closer and closer. And that meant the sword was too. She could almost smell it.

They were nearly halfway down the hall, halfway to escaping this nightmare, when the witches appeared. Swarms upon swarms of them seeped through the walls and out of the darkness. They dropped in front of them and in back. There must have been a hundred, if not more. And they had them surrounded.

The Order froze in their places, their faces dropping.

"Shoot," Meadowrue uttered.

Rose held her torch tight as a voice barreled through her head. *You're never going to make it*, it said, and she knew the voice wasn't her own.

"What do we do?" Eo cried.

"Um . . ." Coram kept saying, glancing back and forth. "Um . . ."

The witches closed in, tongues lolling out of their mouths. Their arms were extended, hands open in anticipation. They made strange little sounds, something that could have been language, and Rose wondered which of them was calling dibs on her. Chest heaving, she held the torch like a baseball bat, ready to swing. She wouldn't go down without a fight. As her fingers tightened around the torch, she felt it begin to rise up out of her hands. But this time it wasn't the witches. It was Ridge.

"Go," he said, and he didn't yell. For only the second time since Rose had been in Eppersett, his voice was soft. He wasn't quiet in prayer like before, reaching far into his family's history. This time it was like he was at peace. In the middle of all this madness, he had found what he had been searching for all his life. He sounded like a different person. "To the door," he said.

Rose watched him raise the torch high above his head, the flames tickling his branches. "Ridge, no," she said, the words barely escaping.

But she could have shouted it and he wouldn't have listened. The fire took hold quickly and spread even faster. In seconds, Ridge was a tree with a full bloom of bright orange flames. He placed a hand against Coram's chest and moved him aside.

"Ridge . . ."

"It's been fun, friend. Gotta run."

Then, with a yell, he charged toward the door, plowing straight into the witches. The Order followed right behind, and because the witches were packed so tightly into the narrow hall, their bodies practically atop of one another, the fire spread wildly, jumping from body to body. Coram and Meadowrue cut a path through the burning witches, as Eo's spikes carried more into the fray.

But Rose saw none of this. Looking behind her now, she only saw Ridge. He was fully engulfed. Every part of him burned, but still he fought, dancing up and down the hall so that no witch remained untouched. His branches reached out, attacking every one they could grab, both in front of him and behind. He was screaming the kind of scream when one knew the end had come, but had not given up the fight. And as he blackened in the fire, arms swinging, branches flying, Rose thought she could see him looking her way. They locked eyes for just a moment, his charred face both hopeful and sad, and it was as if her heart were cleaved wide open.

By the time they reached the red door, the hall was full of flames and in the middle was nothing but a black stump. Ridge was gone, a legend in his own time.

CHAPTER 29
THE CASTLE OF WITCHES, PART THREE

With a punishing blow, Coram kicked the door open and staggered through into the dark chamber. Eo and Meadowrue spilled inside only seconds after, while Rose was the last to enter. When she did, she saw two things. One was the sword of Tarr; the other was a red witch.

"Bahgdaal," she said, recalling the story of Deedubs battle with her in Widcrook. Beside her, Eo was growling in a way that turned Rose's blood cold. It was guttural and thick, drool oozing between his teeth, the hair on the back of his neck sticking straight up, nothing but vengeance in his eyes.

The witch, however, hardly moved. Her skin was heavily wrinkled, the creases so deep the red had become rust. Thick rungs hung off her arms and from her face, pulling everything down. Her body was hunched far over, her spine like a weak branch bearing rotten fruit. Wheezing, she looked old and tired, her eyes dry and unblinking. But still she was smiling as if she knew something the others did not.

With a nod from Coram, the Order spread out within the room, weapons at the ready, waiting for the right moment to strike. All the while, Rose's heart was beating fast, sweat dripping down her face, her legs about to give.

Your luck has to run out sometime, doesn't it? The voices in her head were becoming more and more distorted. She didn't know what thought was hers anymore.

Bahgdaal brought her face close to the sword of Tarr. The final weapon in the group's search was stuck in the dark floor in the center of the room and was the sun they all gravitated around. It was broad and shining, the steel almost transparent—little specks of flame danced up and down within the blade like living things. It bore an intricate gold hilt full of ancient symbols and was almost as tall as Bahgdaal herself. Beside it, her face inches from the steel, she stuck out her tongue. The moment the black tip flicked against the edge of the blade, it was set aflame. Pulling back, without so much as a flinch, Bahgdaal brought her fingers to her tongue and snuffed the fire out. Then she laughed something like a hoarse bark.

Meadowrue's response to this madness was to launch an arrow right at her face. It was fired in less than two seconds and cut through the air at an even faster clip, but Bahgdaal calmly waved it away as if it were nothing but a foul stench. The arrow shifted around her and continued on as if it came out the other side of her skull. A foot from the wall, it turned and came back, aiming to strike her from behind. As if sensing this, Bahgdaal reached behind her and snatched it out of the air, an irritated look falling across her face. Opening her palm, she inspected the arrow over closely, perhaps realizing its power. Looking to take flight again, it trembled in her hand as if wounded. She blew on it, and the arrow bolted from her palm and returned to Meadowrue's quiver, like a frightened child running home to its mother.

Rose watched this and swallowed hard. Meadowrue glanced down at her bow, stunned at its ineffectiveness. Coram's grip tightened on his sword, and Eo's tail lowered, doubt creeping into his eyes.

With a speed that betrayed her age, Bahgdaal's hands shot out and the four of them flew back against the walls.

They slammed hard, and hanging there, Rose's body tightened, like it was constricting into a single point. Defenseless, she felt her bones crunch and her skin shrink, squeezing her insides flat. Her head lowered against her chest, her knees pulled up, her shoulders in. Her ribs felt as if they closed around her heart, her stomach churning. She was a ball of pain and the pain was monumental. Yet, within her head she heard only laughter.

Across the room, Eo's spikes fired from off his back. They came at Bahgdaal from all sides and as her hands waved with a counterspell, the four of them dropped to the floor. Rose landed hard, the breath leaving her body in one quick burst. Orange Blossom left quickly too, darting out from under her shirt and scurrying into a corner. As Eo screamed about taking Bahgdaal's eyes, Rose clutched the ground and looked past them at the sword. They had to reach it, but there seemed to be no way of getting past the witch.

As Rose slowly regained her breath, she thought about using her voice, but Coram's warning flared in her head—she would need everything she had for the Abomination. A hand went up to her throat, scratching at it. The white of the disease had nearly reached it now. It crawled up past her chest in thin strands, reaching, stretching, for her one true weapon. Her throat began to burn, and quite soon, she realized, it might not matter whether she conserved her power or not.

The castle continued to tilt, the ever-increasing wind hammering away, knocking everyone off balance. Bahgdaal, meanwhile, glared at Eo, a look of familiarity in her bulging eyes. "You're his boy," she said with a smile. It was the first time Rose heard her speak, the first time she had heard any of the witches speak so clearly, and the voice sounded almost artificial. Like, after thousands of years, she had finally forced the evolution of language off her tongue.

Enraged, Eo roared and fired his spikes again, but this time Bahgdaal waved her hand and disappeared. A moment later, she appeared beside Eo and sliced open his leg with a blue glow from the tips of her fingers. His body buckled and crumbled, and then she disappeared again, before his spikes had even returned to his armor.

The entire castle was shaking now. The howling wind cracking open the walls, the light and rain seeping in, though Bahgdaal hardly noticed. She was busy spinning Meadowrue through the air, around and around and around, until she smashed her face-first into the floor. With her opponent wounded and vulnerable, Bahgdaal scurried over, hands poised to kill.

Coram charged the witch, his sword raised high over his head. As he leapt through the air, seconds from delivering a punishing blow, he was frozen three feet above the floor. He hung there, and no matter how hard he tried, he was unable to move. Bahgdaal circled him, that deep bark of a laugh escaping her slit of a mouth as she observed her work.

Finally, she said, "I tire. I tire with all of you." Then, holding Coram aloft with one hand, she waved the other.

Even over the noise that had leaked in from outside, a ripping sound could be heard as Coram's skin began to slowly peel from his body.

Bahgdaal twitched a finger toward Meadowrue, freezing her in her tracks. There was a look of surprise on the fairy's face, as some unseen force yanked her backward. Rose heard a strange sound come from her friend's body, a tugging sound, like a tree being pulled from the ground. Meadowrue's hands reached desperately for her back, fingers tracing the stumps of her wings as their deep roots were being pulled from her body. Her head reared far back, and she cried out in agony.

Eo fired his spikes in defense of his friends, and Bahgdaal twitched three fingers in response. The spikes stopped in midair and changed course. They flew right back at Eo, entangling him in their golden cords, squeezing his body tight. Like the deadliest of snakes, they kept constricting, cutting deep into his skin. Eo, unable to stand, fell to his side. He tried biting at the cords, but soon his snout was wrapped shut, nothing but a sad whimper escaping.

Bahgdaal glared at Rose as if daring her to do something. Anything. Rose, however, could only look down in shame. The witch laughed, turning her attention back to the destruction of her enemies.

Backed against the wall, Rose had never felt so helpless. Watching her friends suffer, she couldn't bear it another second. In that moment, she cared for nothing else. She didn't care about her illness; she didn't care about what the witch might do; she didn't even care about the Abomination. She just cared about helping. And so she cried out, a spirited song, and the sword of Tarr wobbled in the floor.

Bahgdaal's head snapped in her direction. It was clear she didn't know what Rose was doing. Confusion shadowed her face, her spells weakening. Even though her throat was on fire, Rose sang with even greater intensity, watching as the weapon slowly rose up behind the witch. With the will of her voice, she turned it, aiming the tip right at Bahgdaal. Finally, the witch realized what was happening. "The Unwonted," she uttered. Closing her hands, she shut down the spells she had placed on the Order and turned her full attention to Rose. When her hands shot back open, her fingers were burning with a new, powerful spell. Rose knew it was now or never. With one final note, her body completely draining of what little strength she had left, her hands writhing before her, controlling the sword, she drove it straight through the witch's back. Bahgdaal's eyes widened in shock as her hands wrapped around the blade. In a flash, she was engulfed in flames. Dropping where she stood, she writhed on the ground as strange words flew from her mouth. Rose knew she was cycling through all different types of spells, desperately trying to quell the fire, but the flames only intensified. This was no lick of the tongue. This was the sword of Tarr straight through her black heart.

Bahgdaal disappeared, then reappeared somewhere else in the room, the sword still burning a hole in her chest. She did this over and over again, but the flames continued to grow. The smoke that filled the room was as red as her skin, and it found the cracks of the castle and leaked outside like a tragic announcement.

Stepping forward, with his gold skin in its rightful place, Coram pulled the sword from Bahgdaal's body, raised it up, and finished her off. Cut in two, she crumbled into a pile of red ash.

Dropping the weapon in exhaustion, Coram turned back to Rose. She was collapsed against the wall, her body starving for breaths, Orange Blossom licking her face. He rushed over to her, fear in his eyes. "Rose!"

And that fear intensified when the ceiling cracked wide open, the storm breaking through, the rain pouring in and the wind sweeping through the halls, spreading Bahgdaal's ashes far and wide. All around them the castle began to crumble. Piece after piece came falling down, a large chunk of dark material smashing just beside Rose's slumped body.

"It's all going to come down!" Meadowrue cried. Her stumps were still in place, though they protruded even more now.

"We have to get out of here," Eo said, his body marked with deep gashes, like long rivers of blood.

Coram bent down and helped lift Rose. There was little life in her, her body deadweight. She only had enough strength to put her arm around his shoulders while he took care of the rest. She had always wanted to be swept off her feet, but not like this. Not like this.

They hurried out into the hall, racing past Ridge's charred husk. Rose glanced back, a weak hand reaching out as a large brick fell from the ceiling and crushed what was left of her friend.

The walls were coming down fast all around them. Holes opened up in the floors. Steps crumbled beneath their feet.

"The Abomination's here!" Meadowrue cried.

Coram pulled Rose closer to his body. He spoke low and with deep concern. "Rose, your voice . . ."

"I'll be fine," she lied. "I didn't use much."

"Rose, we need you at your strongest."

"You're right. I guess I shouldn't have saved you," she croaked.

Coram shook his head. "You're all that matters."

"Just say thank you, you idiot."

Coram smiled. "Thank you."

As he carried her down the stairs, arching his back over her, protecting her from the falling debris, she eased her head against his chest. But even with all the danger around them, she couldn't shake the feeling that he was staring at her. It was like she was back at school and had done something stupid. But she didn't burn up in embarrassment; she didn't cringe at the attention. Instead, her eyes rose up and met his. The look he gave her was so strong, so powerful, that Rose knew she would never fear anyone's gaze ever again. "When I'm gone," he said to her, "I hope I dream. And when I dream, I hope it's of you."

Rose closed her eyes and thought that if she had to, she'd dream for the both of them. It was all she had left now.

By the time they reached the door, the castle was ready to come down. They raced across what was left of the bridge, leaping over huge gaps, and when they looked back, the pyramid came to pieces, chunk by large chunk falling into the water, waves crashing to the shore.

They were safe, but it was only a momentary safety. There was no time for relief, no matter how battered and bruised they were, no matter how tired and scared. They were in the middle of a storm now, and this dark and terrible storm brought with it a tremendous sea of white. It surrounded them, engulfed them. A hundred white shapes.

The Abomination's satellites were waiting.

CHAPTER 30

A STORM OF SATELLITES

"The Abomination has planned for this moment," Rose said, back on her feet, the monster's thoughts so clear in her head it was like having two minds. "That's why we haven't encountered any satellites since Summercress Castle. Instead of sending them out one or two at a time, it's been saving them for one last line of defense. An army to finish us off once and for all."

Coram, his face grave, turned to Meadowrue and Eo and said, "We can't let them get to Rose."

"I've come this far," Rose told him, pulling him around so that they faced each other. "I can handle myself." But as she said these words, her legs gave out beneath her. She crumbled to the ground, her knees lost in the thick mud, her body shivering in the icy rain. It was difficult to keep her eyes from rolling back in her head, the disease taking a forceful hold.

Coram kneeled before her. "I know you can. But you're not well. You need your strength. No matter what happens to us, Rose, you have to move on to face the Abomination. If we die now, you take our weapons, and you do whatever you can to stop it. Understand?"

It wasn't what Rose wanted to hear at all. She didn't want talks of death or of being on her own. Where was the confidence Coram had carried all this time? Where was his faith? Still, she nodded, because she knew it had to be done. The Abomination had to be stopped at all costs, even if that meant she would face it alone.

"We'll do what we can with the satellites," Coram continued. "But you can't be involved in this fight. No magic. I know how well you listened the last time I said that, so I need you to promise me."

"Coram—"

"Rose, without you, Eppersett doesn't have a chance. Your brother doesn't have a chance. So please, for them. For all of us. Promise."

Rose glanced down at her hands—every inch was covered in the disease. Her entire body was now pale white, save for her face. But how much longer before that was engulfed too? And if she didn't stop the Abomination, how long before everyone in Eppersett shared the same fate? She thought of her brother, a lifetime in a bed, alive but not. Locking eyes with Coram, she said, "I promise."

Coram nodded and stood, leaving her with his old sword. Then, facing the coming onslaught, he said, "It's time we finished this."

Before the fight was to begin, Rose dug into her shirt and pulled out Orange Blossom. With both hands, she held the quivering Panatoo level with her eyes and said, "I want to thank you for everything you did for me, Blossom. The company you provided, the support. I couldn't have gotten this far without you. But you have to go now. This is no place for you."

She put Orange Blossom down, but as if stuck in the mud, the Panatoo didn't move.

"Go," Rose said, nudging it along, the rain concealing her tears. "Before the satellites attack. Please. I can't have anything happen to you."

Orange Blossom skittered closer and nuzzled against her leg. It seemed to be whimpering. Biting her lower lip, Rose stroked its glowing bristles.

"I want you to be safe," she said. "There's no need for you to sacrifice yourself. You're free. Go. Find friends. Find your family. Be happy. I'll do everything I can to give you that chance."

Orange Blossom took a few steps to the north, then stopped and looked back, its head low. Rose kneeled there in the rain, shoulders slumped. How was she ever going to succeed when she already felt so defeated? She had said goodbye to Deedubs and Ridge, and soon, whether she succeeded or not, she would have to say goodbye to everyone else. As Orange Blossom's nose twitched, Rose waved and blew a kiss, and as the Panatoo skittered off into the distance, it glowed as bright as she had ever seen it. It carried a warmth and a light she could only wish she would someday experience again.

When it was well out of sight—hidden by a downpour so intense even the orange glow was eventually lost—Rose managed to stand and find her footing, her body wobbling in the thick mud. Ahead in the distance, the satellites were a wide swath of fallen clouds with deep cracks of darkness. She could see the black of their depths as they opened their mouths and widened their eyes in hunger. They were cysts of the Abomination, and they were all sorts of shapes and sizes, one more grotesque than the next. Some were thirty feet tall, while others were the size of dogs and quivering with frenzy.

Some had wings, some had tails, but they all had teeth, and they were sharp and bared.

They came at once, and what was left of the Order bravely met them head-on. It was a clash that blinded Rose's eyes. The gold of their weapons broke through the gloom of the storm like fireballs from the sun. It was a far different reaction than when they had fought Bahgdaal. Here, at the slightest touch, the satellites were in pure agony, and Rose could see why the Abomination so feared these enchanted weapons. Eo's spikes flew in all directions, ripping apart the white of the horizon and spreading its inner darkness across the saturated ground. The black blood mixed with the rain and the mud like a toxic soup, the ground bubbling. Meadowrue's entire body was covered in this mess as she fired arrow after arrow with uncanny speed. They flew straight through one satellite's head and then penetrated the next and the next after that, as if the creatures were indeed nothing but clouds. The steel of Coram's sword was lost in a column of fire. Whenever it was swung, the flames dragged behind it, a wave that carried and crashed against the satellites, shriveling them into black goo.

Rose watched in awe and pride as the enemies' numbers dwindled one by one. It was clear her friends had something they were fighting for, something so much bigger than themselves. They couldn't be stopped. It was like they were fifty feet tall. Rose only wished she could help, especially as she felt the Abomination's fear course through her body as if it were her own.

But this thought was knocked clear out of her head when a tail crashed against her stomach, sending her flying and tumbling through the mud. Her breath shriveled up inside her lungs, but she had enough of her mind to realize that if she hadn't sent Orange Blossom away, the poor thing would have been crushed against her skin. On the ground, gasping and clutching for air, she watched as the white monstrosity came her way.

It was in the shape of a crocodile—if crocodiles walked on two legs. It had a huge snout, with many sharp teeth, opened wide in preparation for its feast.

Like a hammer, the mouth came smashing down, missing Rose by mere inches. She had quickly tumbled to the side, her ribs feeling as if they were powder in her chest, and as she continued to roll, the satellite kept snapping at her, the tip of its snout doused in mud.

After the misses became narrower and narrower, she finally remembered she had Coram's sword and quickly unsheathed it. But it was so heavy in her hands and her body was so weak that she could hardly hold it or herself upright.

Her arms kept sagging, her legs unsteady, and the satellite saw this. Knowing it had her, it slowed its movements, picking exactly how and when it would finish her off.

Rose swung the sword pitifully, all her strength seemingly having left her body. She thought about using her voice again, but hesitated. Right now, she wasn't even sure she would be able to find the breath to produce a squeak.

The satellite neared and Rose was able to cut a gash in its leg, but this only seemed to agitate the creature even more. It swiped at her with its tail a second time, sweeping her legs and knocking her on her back, the sword flying and sinking within the mud. In a flash, the satellite was atop her, claws digging deep into Rose's shoulders. It dragged its razor-like nails all the way down her chest, and Rose was disturbed to see how dark the blood was. The disease had turned it black— what was it doing to her? She wanted to scream, in both pain and horror, but she feared what might burst forth. Instead, she kept her mouth closed and reached for the sword. Her hand dug through the mud, desperately trying to find it. Above her, the satellite licked its lips.

Rose kept searching, her fingers rising in and out of the mud. The satellite dropped forward, its face now inches from hers. Its warm breath wafted across her skin, drool falling on her cheeks like dense rain. The creature's weight sank her deeper and deeper into the ground. It was then that she realized it was going to drown her first. It would feed on her body only when she was dead.

Rose felt herself lowering into the soft ground. Inch by inch, the mud rose up, slowly covering her face. Within seconds, her mouth was buried, her eyes. Then her nose. Still, she reached out blindly for the sword, her hand thrashing into the muck. Everything had gone dark, and the weight atop her was unbearable. Her nostrils filled with mud, her mouth stuffed with it. She couldn't breathe. And through it all, she heard the Abomination's laughter echo within her head.

That was until the tip of her middle finger traced something in the muck. The sword? Her mind searched in the dark of the earth, and it saw the dulled hilt and the battered blade. It was just out of reach. Stretching out—it felt as if her shoulder were about to pop free of its socket—her hand grabbed hold of the sword. Gripping it tight, she found some hidden reserve of strength—like some untapped well in her heart—and, unable to see her target except for in her mind where it was crystal clear, raised the blade and thrusted, gutting the monster open. She knew she had killed it, but there was only one problem. A second later, the satellite's lifeless body fell right on top of her.

Crushed, Rose kicked and flailed in panic, but it was impossible to move it—the weight was just too much. There was no way to get to the surface, to air, and the light in her mind was beginning to fade. Desperate, she screamed—her voice would save her—but her throat was clogged with mud. *This is how it ends*, she thought. *Not with a bang, not with a whimper, but with silence.* And then she apologized. First to her brother and then to all Eppersett.

The darkness came, filling what was left of her short life. It spread over everything, over her past, over her memories, over her mind. And out of that terrible darkness came something even darker and far more terrible. The Abomination. It filled the space of her fading life and swallowed her whole. She could feel it. She was deep within its belly. Again, she tried to scream. She screamed with everything she had. She screamed for life.

And then there was light.

There was air. Wind. Water. There were her friends.

They pulled her up out of the mud, the air ferociously rushing back into her lungs like life itself. She gasped, her eyes thrown wide open, her chest heaving. She felt Coram trembling as he embraced her. She felt Eo's snout nuzzling against her side. And she felt the gentle kiss Meadowrue placed atop her head. They had chased the darkness.

"They're gone," Coram said. "There's not one left. These weapons . . . they're incredible. We can finish the Abomination, Rose. We just need you to lead us." He wiped the mud from her face and eyes. What he saw made his face slacken in fear.

Rose tried to speak but found she couldn't, not even after she vomited up piles of mud. She grasped at her throat, rubbing it. Something wasn't right. It felt as if her tongue had fallen out. Her friends watched her closely, great unease in their eyes. Fearfully, Rose felt her face. Without even being able to see, she knew the disease had spread past her chin and over her mouth. Her body flooded with panic.

"Don't worry," Coram said, though his voice betrayed his own words. "We'll find a way. We'll find a way."

Rose could tell by his eyes he wasn't exactly sure they would. But he had hope. And maybe that was enough.

When she finally got to her feet again, her eyes fell on the distance, where the satellites once were. But now instead of all that white, she saw nothing but black. Immediately, she recalled the darkness of her near death, how all-consuming it had been. What she saw on the horizon was exactly what had invaded her mind in those moments. As the darkness on the horizon neared, her neck kept stretching back and back and back, as her eyes tried to take it all in. It was too much. Far too much.

Panicking, she stumbled backward and fell, her mouth producing nothing but gasps and chokes. Her body vibrated with a fear she had never before experienced. Even her friends slowly backed away, their mouths agape. In seconds, they were all smothered in the blackest of shadows. The abyss of all abysses.

The Abomination had arrived.

CHAPTER 31
THE ABOMINATION

It towered over them, a bubbling black mass that crushed Rose's soul flat. The Abomination: a mammoth shadow in which the faint glow of hope had been all but snuffed out. It was so large, so imposing, that it was as if the night sky had fallen right atop the Order. Gazing up, Rose once again felt herself sinking lower and lower into the ground, her heart already down below her feet. The Abomination had to be over three hundred feet high and almost three times as long. It had legs like an insect, plunging deep into the earth and pulling its massive girth along while white pockets burst all across its back—they were like volcanic eruptions spewing forth premature satellites to defend its master after the army had failed. Although it could have been a monstrous and mutated beetle or bug, it had no eyes, no face. Just that pendulous snout that would eventually engulf Rose.

It plowed forward across Eppersett, accompanied by gale-force winds and torrential rain. The ground behind it was dead, sucked dry of all life. Nothing existed beyond it, and if Rose couldn't defeat the Abomination, it would only be a matter of time before nothing existed before it either.

Like the tiniest of ants, the Order stood before their tragic destiny. Ever since she had arrived in this world, Rose knew the Abomination was a threat, but she had never imagined this. How does one take down something so large? There was no way they could do it. Not with all their weapons, not with Rose at full strength. It was futile. A dream.

And yet her friends didn't seem to share any of these reservations.

"This is it!" Coram shouted over the storm, his breaths heaving from his lungs in huge bursts. "This is what everything has built toward!"

"Our last moments," Meadowrue said, flexing her bow. "Let's make them count!"

Eo glanced up at the dark sky and shouted, "Pa, I'm coming!" And with that cry, a bolt of lightning struck the ground, an electric charge running through them all.

The Abomination carried the storm on its back, thunder roaring overhead in clouds of nuclear winter. With each plunge of its legs, the ground quaked, vibrations stretching for miles. The wind and rain ripped up the land, making it that much easier for the Abomination to consume what lay beneath. Buried in the ground, the snout sucked and fed, and the Abomination grew.

And yet, without a moment's hesitation, Coram called on the Order to attack. Watching as they raced forward, Rose admired their bravery, but feared it was all for naught. She had never felt so vulnerable—so defeated—as she did standing in the shadow of the Abomination. Already, she was its victim.

Her friends were specks of color against the darkness, and she was sure their weapons would induce nothing but the tiniest of pinpricks, an elephant being stung by bees. She watched Coram charge ahead, his sword aflame, the winds so great he was nearly blown aside. When he reached the Abomination, he thrust his weapon into its dark body, a war cry punctuating the attack. As he stood back, pulling the sword free, a pop of light emerged from the wound. It was tiny and hardly noticeable—a white dot that quickly closed up. The Abomination didn't even notice. Seeing this, Rose felt a chill run through her body. It was like the enchanted blade hadn't done a thing. She could tell how frightened Coram was by this too. How he just stood there, frozen, looking dumbly at his sword, as if everything had been a lie.

The Abomination continued to creep forward, pulled ahead by its eight legs, its gargantuan body rising up, ready to fall and crush the disillusioned Coram, who stood defeated in its path. But just as it was about to come down on him, a strange thing happened. A crack of white light slowly spread up from the wound. It traveled across the Abomination's body, zigging and zagging like a fracture, all the way up to its head, and when it got there, the creature reeled back as if in unbelievable pain, a deep bellow escaping its snout like a death knell throughout the land.

A crack of thunder sent tremors through the wind, and the rain came down even harder. Lightning tore up the ground, trees were launched like missiles, and the Abomination writhed.

It worked, Rose thought, rising to her feet. *It worked!*

Coram's eyes returned to his sword, his face slack in stunned awe. Finally, he realized what had happened and darted clear of the Abomination's falling mass. Raising his weapon up so that the others could see, he cried, "Attack!" His voice was shaking with astonishment, the path forward finally clear. "Don't stop! We can do this! We can bring it down!"

Eo and Meadowrue quickly joined in, their spikes and arrows plunging deep into the Abomination's body and tearing it apart. White fissures appeared all over its skin, and an unnerving roar rattled the earth. In that moment, Rose couldn't see her own face, but she knew what was happening by the feeling coursing through her veins. With every blow, the disease was retreating. The Abomination's pain was her medicine. Her friends were doing what they were destined to do: setting up the battle that could be finished only by Rose. The pain in her throat lessened. Her fingers traced her mouth and down her neck as the color returned to her face. Hopeful, she tried to speak, but nothing came out. Her voice was still muted. They had to go faster.

Lightning continued to strike the ground, and it was almost as if the Abomination itself were aiming the bolts. While Meadowrue and Coram were able to dodge these attacks, however, Eo was hit dead-on. He crumbled to the ground with a yelp, smoke rising from his body. He lay quite still a minute—enough for Rose to go completely numb—but then he was up again, the armor having absorbed most of the blow.

The satellites continued to pour forth from the Abomination's body at an alarming rate, but they emerged small and weak. Rose figured they must have been produced so quickly they didn't have time to mature within the darkness. Few were fully formed. Most were missing an arm or a leg, eyes or a mouth. The Order fought them off easily enough, but it left them distracted and tired, vulnerable to the Abomination's attacks. On the defensive now, it had grown long spiked limbs—they could have been stingers, Rose realized—and they were thrust at the Order as if from the tails of colossal scorpions.

As the earth split open, Coram was knocked to the ground, and a stinger came spiking down for him, aiming to pierce his chest and finish him off. He rolled at the last second, and when the stinger impaled the ground, he chopped it in two. The Abomination howled, its body streaked with white veins as the weapons struck it over and over again. "It's weakening!" Coram yelled. "It's vulnerable!" He turned to Rose, his eyes widening as he took her in. "Rose, your face . . . your throat . . ."

Everything went silent, the world around her vanishing in a blink. The only sound was of her heavy breaths. Rose knew it was now or never. The disease was in retreat, but her friends couldn't keep the Abomination at bay forever. Eventually it would overpower them, and Rose would be silenced once again. She had to end this now.

She closed her eyes for the briefest of moments, quietly gathering herself. Then, as if one of the lightning bolts had struck her atop her head and coursed all through her body and down to her feet, she sprang forward. She ran as fast as she could, though everything seemed to be happening in slow motion. She raced past her friends, catching the disconcerting mix of hope and fear in their faces. She saw the ground shift beneath her feet, the sprays of dirt from the Abomination's legs, the bits of earth in the heaving wind. She followed each bolt of lightning from its origin to its end, the growth of the satellites, the deadening of the land. And she saw the Abomination. If it had eyes, she noticed them now as they focused on her. It knew she was coming. Its giant maw opened wide just for her, and she knew she was only going to have one shot at this. And in that moment, Rose wasn't scared. She was ready.

Standing before the Abomination, she watched as the snout came down to consume her. In the next few seconds, she would either die or destroy everything in the vicinity, including the Order. Fail or succeed. It was as if her friends had been destined to die all along too. They were the last thing Rose saw, and the moment she did, she knew it was a mistake. In those stretched seconds, she saw everything they had shared together. She saw their entire pasts and what could have been their futures. Her heart left her no other choice. In her final moments, she gathered every last ounce of strength she had and let out a sonic blast. The winds the Abomination had ushered in were nothing compared to what Rose unleashed. In a split second, Coram, Meadowrue, and

Eo were all blown back as if by a shock wave. They flew for miles across Eppersett. They flew exactly as far as Rose needed them to, and when they landed, they landed safely and out of all harm.

As the Abomination's mouth opened above her, Rose smiled. And then she was eaten.

CHAPTER 32

THE SACRIFICE

She was in the belly of the beast.

In a blink, the world around her had gone away. It was like being dead already. The nothingness. The darkness. A girl lost in eternity.

She could feel two things and two things only: the rapid return of the disease and the acids eating her alive. They were burning through her shoes, and quickly.

She had saved her friends, yes, but at what cost? She had exhausted herself. Once again her throat was constricted by the disease, her voice stifled, and even if her friends were safe from a blast she could no longer produce, they were likely to die a much slower death at the hands of the now victorious and rampaging Abomination. What had she been thinking?

Rose wept.

All her life she had been faced with threats, with struggle and opposition, and they always seemed insurmountable to her. But this was something else. This made those other problems pale in comparison, and she wondered why she ever ran away in the first place. What was so difficult about those battles back home? Why didn't she ever fight back? Was she not alive? Did she not have her health, her wits, her whole life ahead of her? Her problems were nothing like this. They could have been overcome. They *should* have been overcome.

In the stomach of the Abomination, Rose felt incredibly small. She felt weak. A victim. The monster had both silenced and consumed her. And after all she had struggled through, there was nothing left to fight with. She wished she could run, but even that option was gone. She had let down her brother after all. She had let down all of Eppersett, and her friends too.

The darkness and the acids ate at her.

What's wrong with you, Rose?

Though she could still sense its rapturous emotions, its celebratory stomp through Eppersett, the Abomination had fled her mind. She was alone again with her own little voice buzzing between her ears.

What is wrong with you?

"What do you mean, what's wrong with me? I'm dying. I failed. Can't you see that?"

You mean you gave up.

"I didn't give up."

No? What do you call this? You didn't even try to destroy the Abomination.

"I can't! I have no voice!"

And yet you're speaking now.

Rose paused. She *was* speaking. The words came out weak and ragged, but they were there. Still, she shook her head. "It's not enough."

Not enough? There's nothing stronger.

"Maybe it used to be. At some point. But I'm sick now. I'm tired. This evil, it . . . it got the better of me."

Through no fault of your own.

"That's nonsense."

Is it? You succumbed. You've allowed yourself to be consumed because you're too scared to fight back.

"I'm not scared! Maybe I was when I first arrived in Eppersett, but I've come a long way since then. I've seen unimaginable things, and I've fought the whole time. I've fought all kinds of monsters. I fought my way here, to the place everyone else had fled. I willingly sacrificed myself to the Abomination, so don't tell me I'm scared! I'm through being scared!"

Then prove it.

"I . . ."

The disease can be overcome, Rose. It's a weakness feasting on your strengths, and you can't allow that.

"But what am I supposed to do?"

What you've been doing. Fight! Fight now, or your whole life will have been for nothing! Fight for your brother, Rose! Fight for your friends! Fight for Eppersett! Just, whatever you do, don't be silent anymore!

Rose closed her eyes and she noticed a light in her darkness. It was dim, but as she traveled toward it, her body was warmed by its expanding glow. It washed away her fever. There were no fears of death, no regrets or doubts. A small bubble built in her throat, and she said, "This fight isn't over yet."

She knew she had to overcome the weakness that plagued her body and to do that she needed to find an inner strength, some hidden reserve that would pull her through. And so she sought it out in the only place she thought it might be hiding. With reckless abandon, she ransacked her memories, every flash frame of her past, every moment of childhood wonder.

And there she found her brother. She found her mother. She found her father and her friends, her hopes and her dreams. She found all this and more.

Slowly, she began to vibrate, the white light of her inner darkness seeping through her skin. It emanated from every pore, little pops of illumination. The glow grew and grew and grew. A blinding light that turned the Abomination's insides pure white. And then she really began to fight. The light traveled from her chest and up her throat. It rolled across her tongue and between her teeth and across her lips. All she had to do now was give it a push.

And in that moment, she gave it the biggest push anyone ever could. A burst of air came barreling up from her lungs, and her voice rang out like the clearest of bells. The light that had been trapped inside her body expanded outward, not just from her hands, but from everywhere. Growing and growing and growing, feeding off the power of her voice. Soon, it encompassed everything, the Abomination overwhelmed by its force. It tried to fight it, but there was no use. Its body expanded along with the light until both light and dark exploded, the glow of Rose's power overtaking everything. Life as she knew it had become nothing but light. It was everywhere. It was everything. In humble amazement, she watched it consume the world. And finally, it consumed her too.

Chapter 33
AWAKENINGS

Rose awoke in the middle of a forest. She was lying face-down in the dirt, spitting whatever she could from her mouth. As she got to her knees, she recalled what had just taken place and ran her hands all over her body to make sure she was really alive. She looked at one side of her hands, then the other; she lifted her shirt to check her stomach; she lifted the cuffs of her pants to check her legs. The disease was gone. Relief washed over her.

Glancing around, she was happy to see that Eppersett had survived along with her, though she couldn't explain any of it. It wasn't supposed to go like this.

It wasn't until she got to her feet that she realized she

wasn't in Eppersett anymore. She knew these trees; she knew these paths. These were the woods by her house. She was home.

With unrelenting fluttering in her stomach, she was off and running. It was dusk, the night slowly slipping over the sky like a blanket. Without having any clue where in the woods she was, she was somehow able to find her way out with no problem at all. There was no hesitation, no wrong turns, nothing. It was like something pulled her out of there.

Clear of the woods, her feet hit the pavement of the street, and she tore down the road for her little pink house. Usually, she took as long as she could to get home. But right now, she couldn't go fast enough.

Seeing her house again sent a thrill spiraling down her spine. It had never looked so good. *You're a beautiful home*, she thought, and giggled at how happy she was to be alive. She ran across her brown lawn, staring up at her crooked bedroom window. It was called a witch window, she remembered, so that witches couldn't ever get in, and reflecting on the horrors of the pyramidal castle, that made her even happier.

Up the cracked front steps, she threw open the door. "Mom!" she yelled, an aching yearning in her voice. "Mom! Dad!"

But there was no answer. She cut through the living room and checked the kitchen, then the bedrooms. How long had she been gone? she wondered. She glanced at the clock, the X's on her mother's calendar. A day had passed. She didn't know how that was possible when she had spent so much time in Eppersett, but that wasn't her concern right now. She was home. She was alive.

"Mom!"

There was a good chance her parents hadn't even noticed she was gone, she realized, what with all her mom's running around, the craziness that was her life, and her dad's own disillusionment. They never spent much time together anymore; it just wasn't possible. Her mother said they were often like ships passing in the night, and Rose thought there was nothing sadder. How badly she wished she could see her mother right now. How badly she wished her father could be his old self again.

And then, with a magical tingle in her ears, she heard a car pull up, headlights drifting through the living room window, cutting across the wall, then quickly dying. A smile broke out across her face as she ran to the window and looked out. "Mom! Mom!" She was surprised to find herself near tears. It was like her mother had heard her calling.

Really, she was probably stopping home for a quick something to eat before her night shift at the hospital, but Rose didn't care what the reason was. She was home.

Rose threw open the front door, leapt every step of the dilapidated porch, and ran down the driveway, practically tackling her mother before she could even fully get out of the car.

"What's going on?" her mother asked, holding her tight. She kept squeezing, then pulling back to look Rose in the face, then squeezing again. "You haven't left me any messages. You know I don't like it when you don't keep in touch. I get so worried about you."

Rose felt so warm in her mother's arms. She knew how lucky she was to have her. A different mother would have given up long ago. But not her. She was a fighter.

"Mom," Rose said, "I want to go with you tonight."

Her mother pulled back again, gazing lovingly at Rose, a thumb caressing her cheek. "Go? Go where?"

"To the hospital. Please."

A slight twitch cut through her mother's face. "You? Tonight? Rose, you have school tomorrow."

"I don't care; I'll still go. I promise, I won't complain about sleep or anything. Just please, take me. I have to see Hyacinth." The glass of her eyes shattered, and the tears fell. "I just have to."

With a sagging of her face, her mother pulled her in again. "Okay. Okay. Of course I'll take you."

✳

The hospital loomed like the Abomination. To Rose, it was just as dark and just as suffocating. Walking the halls, she felt swallowed. Her body shrank—her shoulders rolled forward, her chin lowered, her arms hugged her chest. It was enough to feel like a little girl again. The smallest of children.

By the time they reached her brother's room, her heart was beating so hard she thought she could see the swell beneath her chest, as if the organ wished to break free and run. She froze outside the door, her face pale, her breaths heavy.

"Are you okay?" her mother asked. "Are you sure you want to do this?"

Rose nodded, her voice slow to emerge. "I need to."

"There's nothing to be scared about. Just think of him sleeping," her mother said. "That's all. It's not like there's a thousand-headed beast in there."

Her mother smiled at her, a twinkle in her eye, and entered the room. Rose cocked her head a moment, pondering over the comparison. But the moment she stepped forward, her mind was washed white. She thought of nothing but what was in front of her.

The room closed in on her, the bed near the far wall, moonlight falling through the window. The constant beeping of the machines found a rhythm in her heart, their tubes hanging like strands of a spider's web. Her feet fell into the patter of her younger self. She approached the bed slowly, thoughts of Queen Sequoia and the prince in her head, their blank faces. She reached the bed, and her mother had pulled a chair for her to sit, but Rose didn't take it. With her chin quivering, she grabbed hold of her brother's hand. It was cold and stiff, the fingers locked.

Her brother didn't look like he was sleeping. He looked like he was trapped, a boy between two worlds. Tubes curled up his nose and in his arms, and he looked small in the bed, as if he had shrunk in size.

Rose tried to speak, but her voice was closed off. Nothing escaped. She wanted to say how sorry she was, though she wasn't sure what exactly she was sorry for. She supposed it was so many things.

His body was suffering, but she knew his mind was still strong. It was fighting. She squeezed his hand tight and again tried to speak. But this time she only let out a quiet sob.

Her mother's hands fell on her shoulders, rubbing them. "Speak, Rose. He can hear you. I know he can."

This is it, Rose thought, and it was as if she were reliving her first visit to this room. *Let him hear you. Wake him up. Bring him home. It's what you fought for.*

She squeezed his hand even harder. She raised her chin. She moved closer, her lips practically brushing his ear. *You can do this.*

With a small burst from her lungs, her lips parted, and she spoke, clear and strong. "I'm here, Hy. It's me, Rose. I'm sorry I've been gone so long. I needed to be stronger for you, like you've always been strong for me. But right now I need you to listen to my voice. Please. If you can hear me, give me a sign. Anything. Let me know you're still there. Let me know you're still fighting."

Trembling, she searched his face for a sign. She watched his eyes, his lips. She kept entirely still, so as to not miss a thing. She refused to blink. She refused to breathe. But seconds passed. Then minutes.

Her mother's hands tightened over her shoulders, and Rose closed her eyes, her throat raw with pain.

Did she actually fail? Was the Abomination still tearing through Eppersett? Is that why the queen didn't follow through on her promise? Or was it all a dream? Did none of it actually happen? Was there no strength in her after all?

She lowered her head, tears dropping on the sheets. A deep sigh escaped her lips. It was time to go. She began to pull away, and that was when she felt her brother's fingers tighten around hers.

CHAPTER 34
FIGHT OR SUCCUMB

Rose had never been so happy going to school. Her father had woken her, and he looked like a new man, his guilt about the accident finally replaced with hope. He had even prepared a grand breakfast waiting on the table. She felt like a new person, one who was ready to conquer the world. It was the feeling she had been waiting twelve years for.

She entered the school, practically throwing the doors open, announcing her arrival. A broad smile was on her face, and she nodded at everyone who was staring at her. Some were snickering, some made comments, but Rose didn't care. She was through hiding. Nothing but life was ahead of her.

Chin up, striding toward her first class, her backpack bouncing on her narrow shoulders, she saw Mr. Fendorf, her favorite teacher, in the hall, lab coat billowing as he tried to remove something taped to the wall. Rose had seen these flyers up all over the place, but in her euphoria she couldn't be bothered to stop and take a look at them. But when she noticed how Mr. Fendorf reacted when he spotted her—the look of both surprise and terror as he quickly tore the paper off the wall—a sinking feeling emerged in her gut.

"Ignore them," Mr. Fendorf said when she reached him. "They know not what they do."

"What is it?" Rose asked, the familiar dark cloud of middle school closing in.

"You . . . you didn't see?"

"See what?"

Mr. Fendorf crumpled up the paper and put it behind his back. "It's nothing. Forget it. Go on ahead to class."

Rose turned her gaze and saw the same yellow paper lining the entire hallway, the entire school for that matter, one every few feet. She walked over to one and pulled it down.

It was a Wanted poster, like back in the Old West, only this one had Rose's picture on it—a horrible one at that—and instead of "Wanted" it said "UNWANTED."

Mr. Fendorf walked up behind her. "We'll find out who's responsible, Rose. I promise. They won't get away with it."

Rose felt her throat constrict. "I already know who it is."

"You do? Tell me. Let us handle it."

"No, Mr. Fendorf. Thank you. But I've got this."

Rose barreled off down the hall. She didn't stick to the walls like she usually did, her shoulder brushing up against the lockers, ducking the crowds and cowering in the shadows of the school. She walked dead center, and this time everyone moved out of her way. She stormed through the east wing of the building until she spotted SallyAnn's locker at the far end. Sure enough, she was there, surrounded by her friends, all of them cackling their heads off in the most obnoxious way possible.

"Sally!" Rose shouted, but it wasn't loud enough. She took a deep breath. "SALLY!"

SallyAnn's laughter cut off as if there were a switch. She glared down the suddenly hushed hall, her brows raising at what she saw. "Rosie!" She slammed her locker closed and made her way closer, shoving two kids aside—the boy and the girl who were holding hands went flying into the lockers—and, arms crossed, stood facing Rose. "It's SallyAnn."

A crowd immediately gathered, pushing in tight. Rose could feel a hundred eyes on her. But she didn't shrink in their presence. If anything, she grew. And not once did her face turn red or her voice go weak. "And you can call me Rose."

"I'll call you—"

Rose shoved the flyer in SallyAnn's face. "You responsible for this?"

SallyAnn lowered Rose's arm, but Rose shot it back up, the flyer remaining an inch from her nose. When she tried it again, the same thing happened.

Finally, SallyAnn said, "It's just a joke. Relax."

From down the hall came the shouts of teachers saying to break it up and get to class.

Rose, a familiar tingle running through her body, crumpled up the flyer and threw it at SallyAnn's chest. This got the crowd humming, and Rose straightened up even more, a slight smirk breaking out across her face.

SallyAnn looked from the ball of paper to the crowd of kids encircling them, her lips stuck in a snarl. She backed away, gesturing to the crowd as if putting on a show. "Little tough girl when you know there's teachers around, aren't you?"

"I'm not scared of you anymore, Sally," Rose said. "I never should have been. You're a joke. A troubled, insecure mess. And if you don't do something soon, you're going to fall apart. And everyone will see it."

SallyAnn looked as if she had been slapped. Her brow furrowed. Her eyes narrowed, her teeth were bared. Fists raised, she charged forward, and Rose didn't move an inch. She didn't even flinch.

Just before SallyAnn reached her, as Rose felt bigger than the Abomination, Mr. Fendorf jumped between them.

"SallyAnn!" he snapped. "Let's take a walk to the main office." He was holding one of the flyers, and as he escorted her away, Rose thought back to the conversation she'd had with her friends about regrets. It felt so good to finally shed them.

Unfortunately, it was during the bus ride home that Rose realized that although she was done with SallyAnn, SallyAnn wasn't done with her. Based on the evil looks being shot Rose's way from the back of the bus, she knew that when she got off at her stop, SallyAnn and her friends were going to be right behind her.

When her stop came, Rose, who had been sitting near the front as usual, climbed off the bus. She made sure to do it at a casual pace, even though her heart was racing. Sure enough, SallyAnn and company departed too, ignoring the bus driver's comments about it not being their stop.

In the street, as the bus idled beside them, they stared Rose down. One of the girls already had her phone out, recording. Rose knew they were only waiting until the bus was out of sight. It was half a minute, but it felt like forever. Then, when it was gone, SallyAnn pointed at her and cried out, "Get her!"

Instinct took over and Rose was off and running.

She knew she had to face them, that it was now or never, but she wanted to do it on her terms. Where she felt safe.

So instead of heading home, she ran straight into the woods.

She found the path but didn't bother to keep to it—there was nothing that frightened her about these woods anymore. The girls' voices trailed her, all vile comments and horrible threats. Rose ran as fast as she could, and it was like the part of her that had existed in Eppersett returned. She was hurdling fallen trees, darting around branches and bushes, leaping over ditches, and little by little, the voices behind her diminished, until they couldn't be heard at all. Eventually, she managed to lose every one of them. All but SallyAnn.

Rose entered a clearing and came to a halting stop—she had run far enough. When she turned around, SallyAnn was standing at the other end of the clearing, facing her. Her chest was heaving, her hair was a mess, her face flushed. Rose had never seen her like that, so unraveled.

"No more running, Rosie. You get what's coming to you," she said, huffing and puffing. "And you get it now."

"You're right," Rose said, her breathing steady as her hands. "I'm done running. I'm never running again. From you or anything else."

"Good. That'll make this easy."

Rose's body tightened. She flexed her fingers as her breathing suddenly intensified. Inwardly, she was searching for the strength she had found in Eppersett. The rise of courage, the flow of power. She would call forth a force SallyAnn could never imagine. Her eyes closed, and she felt that familiar tingle. It spread throughout her body.

SallyAnn stepped forward, a sadistic grin on her face. Her hands were in fists, air shooting from her nostrils like a bull, her eyes locked on Rose. Tossing her head side to side, SallyAnn exaggerated Rose's voice, a sad and whiny tone. "'Please, I want to be in your band! I want a life! I'm a loser and my brother's a vegetable!'" And then she guffawed so hard she bent over.

Rose's entire body was humming with energy now. She extended her arms, a large wingspan, and her fists opened up.

It was like Rose had unfolded the world. She could hear it stretching and pulling. The trees were moving all around her.

SallyAnn heard the noise too, and her laughing stopped. She looked up, a bewildered stammer escaping her mouth. Aghast, she tried to back away but fell right on her back.

Rose never turned around. She didn't have to. The trees moved right past her as if they were her personal army. She could hear them whispering, "She's the one. The sacrifice."

Slowly, they encircled SallyAnn. Rose watched as her tormentor grew small, raising her hands in defense, cowering before the strange sight. "What's going on? What's happening? Rose!"

The trees' branches extended, wrapping around SallyAnn's body. They lifted her high into the air.

"Let go of me!" SallyAnn cried. She was actually bawling now, tears streaming down her cheeks.

The trees carried her back past Rose and out of the clearing. Rose turned around to watch them depart for Eppersett and whatever new danger faced them. Gazing out into the forest, where one world met the next, she saw three figures in the distance. One was on four legs, one had a new set of wings, and the other was gold.

Rose waved to them, her heart twisting up tight inside her, and when they waved back, it unwound so fast she nearly fell down. A part of her wanted to go back, but she knew that it wasn't possible. Eppersett no longer needed her, and she no longer needed Eppersett.

As the trees carried SallyAnn off, Rose heard her desperately call out to her.

"Rose, please! Help! Help me! Rose!"

But Rose didn't help. This was the moment of SallyAnn's struggle. Would she fight or would she succumb? The answer would make all the difference.

THE
END

ABOUT THE AUTHOR

M. P. Kozlowsky is the author of *Frost, Juniper Berry,* and *The Dyerville Tales.* He lives in New York with his wife and two daughters.